HANNA'S PROMISE

A STORY OF GRACE AND HOPE

DAVID CLAIRE JENNINGS

with

JOAN AUSTIN

Hanna's Promise

First paperback edition - first printing, May 2016

ISBN-13: 978-0-9974601-0-0
ISBN- 10: 0-9974601-0-5

Author's website: www.davidclairejennings.com

Photo of Hanna courtesy of Leroy Skalstad, Freeimages.com (portrait of Anne).

The John R. Drish House has been added to the National Register of Historic Places and is registered in the Alabama Register of Landmarks and Heritage. The drawing was captured in 1932. Its author was W. N. Manning. It was accessed through Wikimedia Commons.

Southern Heart Publishing Co.
Liverpool & Athens

For those who came before and made a difference-

Abigail, Harriet, Dilsey and Rosa

Acknowledgments

The prequel to this novel, *After Bondage and War*, was its inspiration. The characters in that work taught us what we needed to know, drove us forward and compelled us to tell the rest of the story. In a generational cycle, the young ones from there become the old ones at the end of this sequel as the new generation lives their lives in America's continuing tumultuous historical times. As some leaves fall and others grow in their place, so too with the generations of flesh and blood, one dies and another is born.

The focal point of *After Bondage and War* was 1865, the end of the Civil War. For *Hanna's Promise*, 1865 is a retrospective reference point.

We end the story corporeally in Ohio where the last one ended but about 40 years later. Spiritually, the story ends simultaneously where it began in Alabama, not far in time or place from Faulkner's imaginary world in Mississippi.

Joan Austin's ear for the southern accent across class, race, region and time – her research into idiom and manner of speech of the many former slaves from the Federal Writers Project – assured authenticity and breathed life into our women's voices in Tuscaloosa and Mobile, Alabama and Mississippi in the late 19th century.

Of the many modern historians produced by Columbia University in the turbulent 1960's under the stern and liberal tutelage of the socialist zealot Robert Hofstadter, Alan Brinkley emerged relatively unscathed. He produced his historiography atypically evenhanded, balanced and without ideological agenda, much in the same manner as the broadcast journalists fading out of vogue at that time. Without the opportunity to have him directly as a teacher, his writings and textbooks provided me an honesty that has kept me from tipping too far in either extreme direction. His *American History: Connecting With the Past, Fourteenth Edition* provides a sound launch point for exploration into any of the vagaries and back alleys of our past we may choose to pursue.

William Faulkner has left us a legacy of America's finest early 20th century writing from our country's own literary canon. Those of us who have had the fortitude to struggle with his enigma and brilliant literary shenanigans, have been rewarded with a richness rarely available to us from the many excellent but more common writers. For the full flavor of "southernness" in all its brutality and humanity in the late 19th and early 20th century, there is no equal. For serious fictional work, and literature at its finest for his readers, his *The Sound and the Fury* published in 1929 and *Absalom, Absalom!* published in 1936, exemplify his immense inspirational value for serious writers following him 80 years hence.

The tradition of American historical fiction has continued into our century. Kate Medina, Executive Editor at Random House recently spoke, as his personal editor and upon the occasion of his passing this year, of E.L. Doctorow and his novel, *The March*, published in 2005. In this, Edgar Doctorow wrote a fresh story of the tried-and-true topic of Sherman's march across Georgia to the sea. She spoke of his talent and humanity and the value of his contemporary writing

Whether it's called a novel or something else, all fictional work, if based on a particular period and its people and events, is historical fiction.

David Claire Jennings and Joan Austin

Contents

Prologue

Long after the cruel war had ended, the Deep South was reeling from its devastation. Its white people were struggling to find a way out of their loss. Its black people were struggling to make a different and better life of their own. The land and infrastructure were destroyed. In their agricultural based economy, cotton continued as their mainstay cash crop. But the world market was declining as other foreign competitors reduced America's share.

Slavery was abolished. African Americans would never wear a slave collar and chains on their ankles and wrists again. They would never be lashed with a whip for saying the wrong word or for trying to learn to read or for leaving the plantation without permission. Their families would not be broken apart and their wives and daughters would not be raped by the slaveholders ever again.

The Republican reformers – the carpetbaggers from the North and scalawags from within the South – were two of the same kind of thing. Both groups were trying to force change in the Southern politics of the Democrats there who were trying to recoup their glorious way of life and undo the defeat of their beloved lost cause. The Southern redeemers there were looking for state and local legislation to circumvent the new 13th, 14th, and 15th Constitutional changes - the so-called Civil War Amendments – while trying to be re-admitted to the government of the Yankees in the Union Federal government up in Washington DC.

Often their adventures were motivated for both good purpose and self-gain. Often for the carpetbaggers, their tools were mendacity and duplicity. Many of them sought graft and enrichment through government control. For the scalawags, especially the vocal ones, like even former Confederate General James Longstreet, their fellow white southerners viewed them as sellouts to their southernness and their great cause for their advocating the new Radical Republican ideas and changes for their country. The Civil War continued with words and politics. Some of the combatants had changed sides. While some lasting positive improvements in education resulted, it was mostly the result of rapid expansion of government services.

In the end, by 1877, they were threatened by the redeemers' violence and repulsed by the stronger southern Democrats. Reform was abandoned. The country once again looked toward the West. By the 1880's, the South fell into quiet desperation.

Share cropping and tenant farming provided something for the freedmen to survive. But they would be economically enslaved and join the poor whites in the meager, but best, agricultural system the South could devise. Bitterness, hatred and poverty would characterize the Deep South for generations to come. Racism would abound after the slaveholders and enslaved parted their ways. Laws would be passed to keep them separate and limit their freedom. But there were glimmers of hope for the races to live together in harmony.

The black Christian woman had come from Mobile, Alabama to McComb, Mississippi to care for the people and their children, keep their houses, and heal their ailing bodies and spirits. She was their Negress but she brought her faith and her love and it spread to those around her.

She was born in Tuscaloosa on a plantation in the sweltering heat of Alabama – born of a young slave woman brought there from another crueler plantation in Mississippi and conceived back there from a slave father lost to her when her mother had been sold.

She had been treated special there in Alabama, maybe out of pity or maybe because the owner was a more kindly man. But it was in the middle of America's time of greatest cruelty and human injustice, nearer the end of it before the great war. It was a hard time in the country.

She grew up as a fatherless child with a loving mother until her mother had been killed. Now, as a complete orphan in the depth of a human tragedy, it seemed as though God had not noticed her, wasn't paying attention or didn't care in that time of America's deepest sinful shame when His people had turned their backs to His intentions. That was true of them, but not Him.

With the help of some kind older people, she was able to survive her childhood and overcome the horrific events of those early years.

God kept His promise when her mother had been killed so long ago; for He was keenly interested in those troubled times and this young life.

Her impact on the people in her life would seem disproportionate to her humble status. Perhaps it was just because of that that her life was so profound.

The South soldiered on long after its men had surrendered. Ignored and on its own, it rebuilt itself and its people endured on its American land.

Illustrations

Hanna Drish in McComb, Mississippi in 1895

John R. Drish House in Tuscaloosa, Alabama

Historical Oberlin College, Cleveland, Ohio

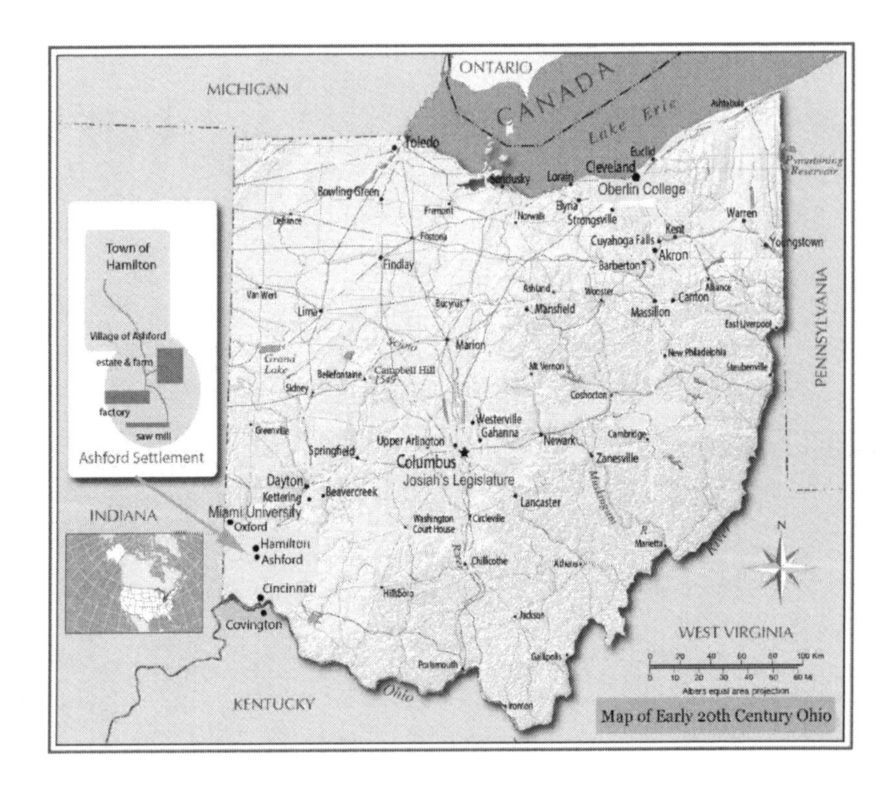

The Ashford Family Ohio Homestead in the 1920's

One – The Twins

Josiah rose from his seat, walked to the podium and shook the speaker's hand. He looked out at the assembly, paused to look across the room and smiled. He stood bolt upright and with his left thumb in his suspenders and right hand raised in the air, spoke to his colleagues.

His face turned to its characteristic resolve as he spoke eloquently and clearly:

"Speaker, esteemed colleagues, we find ourselves at a crucial moment. What we decide today will affect our constituents - our people, our citizens, our families - for the remainder of their lives and for the lives of their descendants to follow.

The great Ordinance of 1787 gave us a plan and guidance to follow. It provided land for schools. The schools were built. But education has been left to us - the great state of Ohio to resolve for ourselves. Much has changed since then; much has run afoul. I will speak to you about that today. We have the opportunity, the authority and the responsibility to change that, correct that and rectify that."

The room was silent in rapt attention. He continued:

"The intent of our founders was clear. We would establish a great nation to the extent of its boundaries, not even known at that time, where free men would live their lives and prosper under the grace of God, as no nation had ever done before."

Loud cheers and applause broke out and drowned Josiah's words. The speaker rapped his gavel for several moments and spoke out, "Attention! Attention! Call to order!"

The room returned to silence and Josiah continued to speak:

"Many of our aspirations have come to pass to fulfill our original ideals. We have turned around the subversions of our southern fellow citizens with the sacrifice of the blood and treasure of our people. Abraham Lincoln brought us to that eventuality and shall ever be remembered for the salvation and redemption of our nation."

The room remained silent in anticipation. He continued:

"Today we have many laws establishing the rights of property owners and for our citizens to vote and hold public office. Our schools are flourishing, our children are benefitting from this, and our country is improving."

They waited for his next words:

"But there is more to be done. There is always more to be done. We will never achieve perfection, but we must strive for it, reach up for it, as Americans and God loving human beings.

We have before us SR403. It will guarantee equal access to higher education for all our children without regard to the color of their skin. It will be based on the content of their character and our character. Surely, honor and integrity will compel us to pass this as the right thing to do. I urge you to vote for it in the affirmative."

Applause broke out one last time as Josiah returned to his seat. Assembly bill SR403 was passed by a narrow margin. It ratified and finalized the senate bill that preceded it. Citizens of all races would attend Ohio's educational institutions. Mary and the children understood that Josiah had played an important part in this change. They were proud of him.

After Bondage and War, Josiah Ashford

The Twins

David and Josena Ashford were born on May 17th in 1870 as the twins of Josiah and Mary Custis Ashford. David was five minutes older than Josena. They were raised in Hamilton, Ohio and for years they had heard the stories from their father, his white friend David and their mother about the past – slavery, the Civil War and failed Reconstruction. They had heard that there was an older half-sister from their father's tragic first marriage in Mississippi.

The twins' names were chosen with care and purpose when they were born. Josiah had wanted to preserve important memories from the past. His wife Mary understood this, and because she loved him so, she lovingly agreed to his wishes for her children. It was not her history, but it was his.

For David Ashford, it was Josiah's abiding friendship with David Wexley, the Union soldier from Baltimore. He had first met him in Natchez at the edge of the Big Muddy when David strolled over to him and asked him who he was.

Josiah had walked over there, just emancipated from the plantation Savannah Oaks nearby to the east. David had walked much farther from the east, just released from the Confederate prison camp called Andersonville in southwest Georgia. By either pure happenstance, or divine providence, they arrived there together the same afternoon within a couple hours of the same time. This chance meeting had profoundly altered their lives. It had set their whole lives on a trajectory of redemption and fulfillment. David would never forget their history or the history of his country.

For Josena Ashford, it was her father's loving sad memory of his first wife, Josena Taylor Ashford and his lost daughter whose life and name he did know. Her father had had a brief marriage when he was a slave in Mississippi. She had been taken away and killed on another plantation in Alabama. It was a poignancy Josena would never forget, as though she had lived the life of her namesake – as though it had been her own life.

As fraternal twins, they had a similar general look about them. They were close comrades of thought throughout their whole lives. But from there they departed.

David grew to be tall and lanky. He was taller than his father but not so big and robust – more wiry. He had a sharp mind and a thirst for learning. After he had done that – learned – he became professorial. He was contemplative and reflective, but once his mind was clear, he would launch into long lectures to teach you what he knew and wanted you to know. He was always careful and skillful to avoid unnecessary confrontation if he thought it served no purpose. He was generally affable and gregarious.

Sometimes he would miss the mark, but was gracious when someone he respected pointed him in the right direction. That would be his sister.

Josena grew to be short and heavy – some would say dumpy. But she was not frowsy. She may have had to look up at you, but was always put together and immaculate, maybe elegant in spite of herself. She had a fat elegance once you got to know her if that makes any sense. It was about her mind too.

She was smart as a whip and self-assured. She never suffered fools gladly and would rip into you if she thought you were misguided or ignorant. David had to hold her back on many occasions for her own good and the good of the circumstance.

Together they reminded you of Abraham and Mary Todd Lincoln, had they not been a brother and sister of color from a more modern time.

They grew up together on a parallel path and supported each other as the alter egos that they were.

The twins began their college attendance in 1887 at Miami of Ohio University in nearby Oxford. The college had been built on land provided by the Northwest Ordinance. George Washington signed for the land purchase from the Miami Indian tribe and the village of Oxford was laid out in the college township. The original purpose of the school was to train teachers, so it was referred to as a normal school.

They took introductory level courses there permitted under a new pilot program for Negroes that showed promise. It was a program urged by their father, Ohio State Congressman Josiah Ashford. But the university had no intention of conferring degrees on Negroes. It was too soon for that precedent and they weren't going to be the first. It wouldn't be until 1905 before Nellie Craig would graduate there as a teacher and the first African American.

When Josie and David learned that they would never be permitted to graduate, they brought their concern to their father. Josie told him the program was a sham. She was more emotional about injustices than David and became more easily outraged.

Josiah was upset, but ever the pragmatist, he counseled them to apply to Oberlin College up near Cleveland. This prestigious college founded by Presbyterian abolitionists would provide them opportunity for any degrees they wished to pursue. Miami of Ohio's time for equal treatment of the races had not arrived in time for his children. Oberlin was more established than Miami and offered the twins a broader selection of courses and degrees. It had worked out for the best.

Josie would never forget the slight she felt from the treatment she and David had received at Miami of Ohio, but would someday become a prominent professor there. She became more pragmatic as she matured.

At Oberlin, providence was kind to the Ashfords. Despite its abolitionist foundation, Oberlin was prominent as a Protestant conservatory of music with a white majority and few blacks.

David and Josena were a curiosity. They were different in the eyes of most of the student body. But as a curiosity, their classmates were drawn to them, not viewed as people to be avoided.

They were recognized as progeny of a prominent family with a father a powerful politician in the Ohio government. And they were Ohioans like Grant from Point Pleasant, the former general and president who had just passed away five years ago. No one viewed them as ignorant Negro farmers from Mississippi or Alabama.

David had a good sense of this and used his affable nature to form many friendships with his white classmates. Josena learned too that her father's advice would be fruitful in forming relationships. They were colored for certain, but in this environment, that could be advantageous. They became that best of all things in college – popular.

When they stood beside each other, it was humorous – two such uneven fence posts. "How could they be twins?" their classmates wondered.

Their campus life grew to a point where they could discuss race openly, and they did so through many a long night of the brutal harsh winters near Cleveland along the southern edge of Lake Erie.

When David spoke of history, they wondered why it was not he, rather than the professor, standing at the front of the classroom.

Josena organized and led an all-woman string quartet to feature the beloved works of Mozart. Her second violin, cello and viola players from Illinois, New York and Maryland were young passionate white girls. And how they loved Mozart. Their music sparkled and filled their artistic souls. When Josena put her bow to the strings of her violin, she fairly took their breaths away. She held them speechless in rapture. Their throats tightened and their eyes shone.

Their college life was gratifying and it was painfully sad when they graduated and had to leave.

After they had graduated college and remained in their home area for a few years, they decided they wanted to travel into the Deep South to see what it had become now. They had learned in college the murmurings of an emergent movement for social justice and civil rights still denied to so many Americans.

And just maybe they might find their lost older half-sister who had been spoken about in such mysterious, almost mystical and even mythical, ways. Their sister's existence was an enigma. No one knew about her with any certainty.

David Ashford was smart. And he was thoughtful and wise beyond his years. He learned early how to observe those around him and how to gain understanding. He learned from his father and mother and from his father's friend, Uncle David. He absorbed all the knowledge available to him.

At Oberlin College he learned about history. He knew that those that didn't know history could not think historically. Without that training, if would be difficult to understand the world and its meanings.

David learned that history study is a discipline that approached understanding like viewing the layers of an onion as they are peeled away. He learned about all the important facts – the events in the Classic, Old World and American histories. With this comes the understanding of the causes and outcomes, as event leads to event in succession. And with those events are the people positioned in power to drive the events – the game-changers. These are the facts, the outer layer of the onion. There is not much in doubt or dispute here. When assembled together, they form the first layer – the information.

With thought, discussion and reflection, David gained insights into the ideas of history as the next layer becomes revealed. Certainly personal perspective and bias begins to creep in with this step, but information becomes knowledge. He is a black man – an African American son of a former slave – and nothing would change that.

Finally, the ideas he considered are merged together to reveal the meanings. Individuals depart to different conclusions here as more perspective is invariably applied. But here, in this inner layer, knowledge ends with wisdom. His college education was more profound for him than some of his classmates because of his experiences in his formative years.

He came to understand that for many, truth is the facts that they choose to love. He knew that it is a mistake to look back at a period in the past and base truth on ideas and values of the present. Only by placing yourself in that past period can true understanding of those past motives, beliefs, events, causes and outcomes be gained. The truth is for those past people, their truth, not the truth of the observer many years after. David understood this as the purpose of history study. It helped him understand the present.

Josena had attended Oberlin College with David and graduated with her brother. She had studied the arts and the humanities. This brought a different perspective to her intelligence. Hers was based on sociology and understanding the nature of human kind.

She studied violin and became an accomplished musician. From the classics of Beethoven, she gravitated to the old sweet American tunes as Jefferson had played them at home in Monticello.

She was a black woman and understood she was different when white people looked at her with the prejudice of Social Darwinism, convinced she was inherently inferior. But she knew better and never suffered fools gladly. She used a sharp tongue when circumstance went beyond her limits.

David and his twin sister Josena had grown up on the Ashford estate in a life of comfort, but not one of ease. There on their land, the successful Ashford Furniture Company assured the family's wealth. But they were black and never at ease.

The region surrounding the town of Hamilton had seen progress in its rural economy and in its societal improvement just in the two decades from 1870 to 1890 as the twins grew to adulthood. It would take many decades more before full civil rights and social justice would be realized. But it would come sooner than in the South.

Racial harmony was an entirely different matter. It couldn't be legislated or forced. It had to come with the change of hearts. Old attitudes had to be unlearned. After the chains of slavery had been broken, the chains of hate remained. The twins knew this and were attuned to it more than their parents.

Racial prejudice was to be found everywhere. It troubled Josena more than David. He listened to her impassioned arguments with their father. Her emotional outbursts to the great man were common in their family life.

"White men are ignorant father. They have no basis for their stupidity", she said.

Josiah, with his wisdom, tried to convince her that her attitude would never resolve it or change it.

He told her, "Never bow or scrape. You are entitled to your pride. You must maintain your integrity. But if you want to change their hearts, you have to kill them with kindness – but by using your intelligence. It takes time. I have seen it work in my life. You know I have made progress in the legislature with the white men I have worked with there. It wasn't just about convincing them to pass legislation. It was also about winning their respect."

And also, "My sweet, beautiful brilliant girl, remember always with pride, our relationship is special because your name is the same as the brave slave woman that was once my wife."

She nodded in tacit agreement. It was something more she would have to learn.

Right from the start, David was reflective and thoughtful; Josena was reactive, impulsive and passionate. Both were resolute.

Two - Hanna

With a clarity of understanding and resignation Joe said, "Yeah, it's too late now for me to find her. But how can I forget her? I can never forget her. As much as my heart aches, I must find comfort in knowing that I have a daughter who was the result of my love for Josie. I can only pray that she will have the kind giving heart of her mother, and that God blesses her life."

"She will Joe, God knows she will."

After Bondage and War – Josiah Ashford and David Wexley

She was born on the Drish Plantation in Tuscaloosa, Alabama in 1856, six months after her mother was brought there and eight years before Josena would be accidentally killed there during the slave revolt. John Drish and his wife had treated her kindly, as they had her mother when she had been bought and brought there.

John Drish gave her her name, Hanna Drish, even though her mother had been Josena Ashford. Hanna's father, Josiah Ashford, knew that his lost wife had had a baby girl before Josena was killed. He lived in the North and was never able to find her. He knew about her but never knew her.

Little Hanna was raised as a house servant like her mother had been. She was a happy baby, not as light in color and without the pristine beauty of her mother. But her little heart and pure soul was all Josena. Her smiling face brought happiness to the Drish household. Without any children of their own, they loved her as their own.

She grew up with the other slave children in the household and on the plantation. There was something bright and spiritual about her – like the glow from the Alabama sunset. It touched the heart of those that knew her. She reached out to others in her special childish way.

Following her mother's lead, Hanna went to work and learned how to help out in the big house and minister to the slaves in their cabins. Together they tended the sick.

As she grew older, she began to ask a lot of questions as children do. She wanted to know who her daddy was, and where he was. Didn't she have a daddy like everyone else?

Josena would hold her close and smother her against her breast. She sang lullabies to her softly, clearly, sweetly:

Them that's got shall have
Them that's not shall lose
So the Bible said and it still is news
Mama may have, Papa may have
But God bless the child that's got his own
That's got his own

and:

Swing low, sweet chariot,
Coming for to carry me home.
Swing low, sweet chariot,
Coming for to carry me home.

I looked over Jordan, and what did I see
Coming for to carry me home?
A band of angels coming after me,
Coming for to carry me home.

Sometimes I'm up, and sometimes I'm down,
Coming for to carry me home.
But still my soul feels heavenly bound,
Coming for to carry me home.

The brightest day that I can say,
Coming for to carry me home.
When Jesus washed my sins away,
Coming for to carry me home.

If you get there before I do,
Coming for to carry me home.
Tell all my friends I'm coming there too,
Coming for to carry me home.

Hanna learned very young that there is so much beauty, solace, forgiveness and truth in faith.

Josena whispered through Hanna's tears that she had a wonderful daddy but he wasn't there with them.

When Hanna grew older, she stopped asking about her father because she saw it made her mother very sad. Hanna had an instinct about people and their feelings. She was like an old soul that had seen so much of life. She tried hard and learned how to make people happy. But for her, it came naturally. She didn't understand yet that God was inside her and working through her.

Hanna noticed the times her mother seemed to be off in another world, one of memories of her life past. During those moments her mother would seem to be silently praying or quietly crying. She intuited that there had been great pain and loss in her mother's life.

Not wanting to see her mother so sad, she would often do something silly to try to make her laugh and forget. Most times she was successful and lifted her mother's spirits. Hanna was learning how to love and make people happy. She possessed a calm and quiet maturity and a wisdom associated with someone much older.

When she was seven years old, on one evening when the day's work was done and Hanna and Josena were alone, her mother drew her into her arms and holding her tight said, "Hanna, time I'se tole you somethin' about your fathah 'n' wheres we's lived. But when I'se done, we's nevah talk 'bout it agin. You understan' chile?"

Hanna was surprised and a little scared. Her mother had never spoken to her like this before. She could see the sadness in her mother's eyes, but at last maybe some of her questions would be answered.

"Yass, Momma" she replied and waited for her mother to speak.

Josena opened her heart as she spoke, "Your fathah was a wunnerful man. I'se love him from de minut' I'se sees him. He's handsum 'n' very smarts – like's you he's question everthin'."

"We jump de broom 'n' be marry by de Savannah Oaks Massa. We's live ina small cabin. I'se work in de house 'n' ya fathah, Josiah, he be a carpenter on de plantation. My lands, you's shoulda seen sum de beautiful furn'ture he make fo' the big house!"

She paused a moment as if deciding how much to tell her young daughter. She had never talked about her life at Savannah Oaks, preferring to enjoy the love and affection she received from the Drishs than to remember the hatred of Rebecca and the betrayal of Marcus who sold her away from Josiah.

But Hanna was getting restless, so she continued her story.

"You's look mo' likes him than me. He's a big heart 'n' a lotta faith in de Lord. I'se done tole you, he's very smart; he's even teached hisself to read", she said smiling quietly to herself. "'N' he done it wid books I'se smuggle out uv de Massa's house."

Like every good mother, she didn't want to burden her child with some of the painful and grownup truths about her own life. So she didn't tell Hanna that Marcus Taylor, the Massa, was her father who had raped her mother, and how hurt and betrayed she felt by her father selling her. She only wanted Hanna to feel loved and protected.

Hanna listened closely and, as an intelligent child, she had another question.

"But momma, where my daddy? Why ain't he be heah wid us?"

The tears flowed quietly down Josena's cheeks as she answered, "He don't knows I'se havin' a baby when I'se sole 'way from Savannah Oaks. Iffen he's knows 'bout you, he's very proud uv you, justs Is'e am. You such kindheart' 'n' lovin' girl. I'se knows you always makes me proud, 'n' him too iffen he's knows 'bout you."

Josena and Hanna sat holding each other quietly for a while. Josena didn't know why she had chosen this time to tell Hanna about Josiah, but she just had a feeling that it was the right time. Maybe God had chosen this time to move His plan along with these human beings.

"Now 'member Hanna, we's ain't nevah goin' to talk 'bout this agin, but you's ole enuf to knows about your wunnerful fathah 'n' whys I sumtime get sad when I'se think's 'bout him 'n' how much we loves each othah."

In another year Hanna's mother would be gone and hell would be on its way to the Drish plantation.

As the war drew to a close in 1864, Hanna was eight years old. Dr. John Drish, and his wife Sarah, brought her to live with a friend in Mobile, Alabama for her upbringing, safekeeping and wellbeing. She was raised there in their mansion where she helped them keep their house and was a companion to their children. She was a member of their white family.

Hanna helped out around the household working with the servants. But she was more like an adopted daughter growing up in her parents' home. She had her own room on the second floor family suite with Ken, Abigail and their two daughters. As was the custom, the live-in household servants had their quarters on the third floor apart from the family.

One night when she was 13 in 1869, she was sleeping in her quiet room. She was having a dream of vivid proportions. She suddenly awakened to the sound of soft beautiful music. In the room, dimly lit with the sputtering light of the oil lamp on the table, a heavenly visage appeared. He was imposing, very tall and magnificent in his warrior raiment.

"Hanna, do not fear. I am Michael from the South of Fire. God has sent me to meet you."

The Archangel of God's second phylum smiled at her and his strikingly handsome African features reassured her. His beautiful coffee colored skin was aglow and lit the room. It was so bright, it was like looking at the sun as it sets on the horizon in the southern sky.

Hanna was calm and at peace. She waited to hear his message.

Michael spoke clearly without equivocation as he began, "God has watched you every day since you were born on the plantation. He was with you the day your mother Josena died. He guided the Drish family and compelled them to single you out and love you."

She sat on the edge of her bed speechless in rapture and awe.

"God knows your pure spirit and has chosen you for a special life to serve Him by ministering to the black and white people of the South. He knows that they are hurting, disheartened, bitter and hateful. He wants you to work through Him and dedicate your life to heal them."

She nodded her head but couldn't believe what was happening.

"This is God's covenant with you Hanna. He will keep you safe from harm from all humans for the rest of your life. You will never marry or have children or a family of your own. Your promise to Him will be to serve Him always by spreading His spirit of true love to all white people and black people you come to know."

He waited for her understanding and response.

"I will", she said simply.

Michael smiled at her and she felt God's warmth through His powerful messenger. He came over to her and held her in his arms.

"God loves you child", he said and disappeared from the room.

Hanna grew up to become a strong woman of purpose who was courageous and resilient. She had no fear of people because she believed God's promise as Michael had spoken it.

Her appearance was plain. Her face had none of the soft smooth beauty of her mother's. It was creased with the lines of care and concern. She had the stern serious expression of resolve like her father. It wasn't angry or unfriendly, but rather formed from the passion of her mind. It was an unfamiliar look for kindness. She lived the words of Micah – act justly, love mercy, walk humbly with your God.

Three - The Drishs and the Blanchards

John Drish came from Virginia. He was born there in Loudoun County near Arlington and the Potomac River in 1795. The county was established from Fairfax County in 1757. George Washington was still President then and it would be two more years before his Vice President, John Adams would assume the Presidency. The District of Columbia was not established and it wasn't until 1800 that Adams became the first President to live there in the President's House. His rival and Vice President, Thomas Jefferson would take over later that year.

He studied medicine at Harvard University in Massachusetts and met Kenneth Blanchard there. Kenneth had studied business. He had come there from his home in Charleston, South Carolina.

John and Ken had much in common and struck up a close friendship from the moment they met. They were both southerners, chums in college and graduated the same year. They were southern gentlemen in the truest and best sense.

Certainly they behaved with refined gentility and courtly manners. They spoke slowly at the same melodious pace, taking their time as though the words really mattered as they flowed from their lips like sweet molasses. The lilt from the rise and fall of their intonation was seductive to the ear with a lightness like the scented breeze through the pines in Virginia and the ebb and flow of the tidewaters in Carolina. That is how it sounded in America. But its roots came long before from their forbearers back in the British Isles.

John and Ken were kind, as well as charming, but never gave a thought about the immorality of keeping human property. Long before them their society had ceased caring about that in the South, and few cared about it in the North either. The incongruity with their Christianity was not apparent.

It was understood that the southern system really began when the English Anglicans came to Jamestown in 1607 and established the first enduring settlement. They were the Royal Cavaliers and thought of themselves more like noble soldiers than farmers.

They had no desire to make a society out of moral piety and build a shining city on the hill for the glory of God as John Winthrop had just sermonized to his Pilgrims as they alighted from the Arabella onto the soil of the New World. The Virginians were ill equipped to suffer hardship in service to their God.

Like the Spanish Conquistadores before them, they came in search of gold and riches in the new land. Many perished when none was to be found and they were threatened with the necessity of having to work with their own hands.

But they did discover something as good as gold. The Indians took pity on their sad helpless situation and befriended them. They taught them to grow tobacco. All they lacked was the labor to do the hard work. The slave triangle system developed with the trading companies and in short order the Virginians profited mightily from their tobacco crops and their dreams of wealth were fulfilled. Tobacco money bought more slaves and more slaves produced more tobacco in an escalating spiral until the soil wore out.

As much as they might have wished to be viewed as conquering knights, they settled for agricultural nobility with their own fiefdoms and peasants. As tobacco profits began to wane in Virginia, rice and indigo wealth arose in the Carolinas. The plantation dynasties had established a firm foothold.

But John and Ken grew up in cities and had no ambitions for vast land holdings and grand plantations to grow cash crops and profit from the sweat of their human property. They stayed up nights at Harvard and talked about their plans for their lives.

"I'll be practicing medicine because it will be my vocation and I want to care for people. But my selfish love will always be architecture", John would say.

Ken would answer, "I know you John and know that's true to your nature and good heart. For me, I'll probably not settle in Charleston. My roots are in the Gulf South. If not New Orleans, I'll be making my life along there somewhere."

John thought about their lives and suggested, "It'll be interesting to talk to each other twenty years hence to see what we did and how the world changed."

Ken sighed, "One thing I'd bet on is that slavery will be abolished. It won't last much longer. Then our beloved South will be changed forever – for the good I believe."

John had a wide range of diverse interests and was restless to get started. He loved artisanship, architecture and machinery. Ken favored the commercial business model of New England mercantilism even though his ancestors had come to Carolina from the Gulf Coast.

After they left college, they didn't see each other for years until they found each other again in Alabama.

When John came to Tuscaloosa in 1822, he built a most unusual mansion on his 450 acre property and operated a most unusual plantation business. He was a widower and came to Tuscaloosa as a man of sorrows. He eventually married Sarah Owen McKinney, a wealthy widow herself in 1835.

He was a slaveholder for certain, but followed the old Upper South tradition of the task system and treated his slaves much better than the hasher treatment they typically received there in the Deep South.

He was a medical doctor, a successful physician, a building contractor, and a plantation businessman, but his passion and avocation was architecture. He designed a unique Greek Revival and Italianade styled mansion with full width monumental Doric porticoes and invested in training his slaves as mechanics, masons, plasterers, blacksmiths, artisans and craftsmen so that their labor would construct his dreams. It was completed in 1837. The University of Alabama was established in Tuscaloosa just before that in 1831. It was mostly destroyed during the Civil War.

An extensive addition was put onto the mansion prior to the Civil War. In 1860, his slave William began construction of a three-story brick tower. The front columns were changed to Ionic and cast iron side porches were added.

His workers ran machinery and he provided a cotton ginning service to the planters in the region who didn't want to gin their own cotton. It was much like farmers bringing their grain to a gristmill facility, but an unusual service for the cotton agricultural industry.

He treated his household slaves as family as long as they conducted themselves as obedient children. His Negroes were never whipped and, with the task system, they were given more free time for their families and their gardens. He never broke up families and sold family members away. There was almost a loyalty in this more benign relationship of human bondage. John was kind and there was mutual affection between the master and his charges. But he was understandably a paternalistic and controlling parent.

When his overseer, John Manford purchased Josena at the auction in Natchez, her background from Savannah Oaks was not known. The slave brokers did not make a practice of bothering to learn or pass on the life stories of the commodity they were selling. John Drish was unaware that Josena had been taken away from her husband, or that she was the daughter of the former slaveholder, or that she had grown up mistreated and abused by the mistress of the mansion where she served, or that she was light with child when she arrived. It would be much later, too late, when he would find these things out.

The Blanchards were Catholics. Their people had come to Charleston from the Gulf Coast French. When they settled there, it was an immutable fact that they were an inferior breed of

Christians in the eyes of the Anglo Saxons. The Carolina people paid more mind to what kind of a Christian you were, not how good of one you were.

After college in Massachusetts, Ken moved back home for a brief while. Then he moved to the Gulf shores to seek his fortune in business. He settled in Mobile nestled in its bay up river from the Gulf.

Ken met Abigail before the war up in Virginia. She had been John's first wife's best friend and was introduced to him through that relationship. When they moved to Mobile, the Blanchards maintained a long distance friendship with the Drishs up in Tuscaloosa.

Ken became a wealthy merchant who made his fortune in the import – export business from the port of Mobile in Alabama. There had been plenty of opportunity before and after the war. Despite the upheaval the war caused, the change in the status of the Negroes, and all the changes in the agricultural system of the Deep South, the cotton business had been steady enough for his purposes.

He owned slaves as domestics and stevedores but 1865 brought them their freedom. Many stayed with him after that and were paid wages for their services. Without further cost for their direct care, it worked out about the same for him. And of course they were free to leave if better opportunity came along. The relationships changed mostly as a matter of perception.

With their emancipation, many of the Negroes were still working where they worked before as slaves, but now they had a way about them as free people – celebrating in gatherings off to the side and out of the scrutiny of the white folks. Cooking food, laughing, singing, playing banjo music and developing their own free culture, poor but glad to be alive and happy for themselves. They were themselves for the first time in America and were nothing but happy for that.

But their war had just begun at the conclusion of the white man's Civil War. They strived to better their lives with education and active participation in suffrage and political office. Their progress was breathtaking at first. But invariably the southern governments took much of it away with the support of the hateful and violent redeemers. The African Americans persevered and endured with steadfast courage. Their rock was their church and their colleges were the promise of their future.

As all men are, they were a product of their time. But their fundamental goodness would be their oar to steer them through the currents and eddies of an uncertain future.

The Drishs and the Blanchards had adjusted to the new realities. They were not selfish and hateful people. Their kindnesses and generosities made life better for the extended families that were part of them. People like them would be the hope for the South as the changes came in the future generations.

John died in 1867 at age 72. He had weathered the storm of war, and its ruin, and managed to help with the rebuilding. He was still solvent from the financial ravages and managed to leave Sarah a life of comfort and ease in his absence. He had fallen down a staircase and was accidentally killed. Sarah lived until 1884. The folklore about them and their home spoke of ghosts and hauntings that would persist for decades.

Ken missed him and their frequent visits between Tuscaloosa and Mobile.

Four- The Slave Revolt

John Manford was upset with his employer, John Drish. Manford was the overseer, but Drish wouldn't permit him to whip the slaves in his charge to keep them in line.

With all John Drish wished to accomplish on his land, with his people, and through his many interests, all did not go perfectly with the approach he had taken. Many of his slaves had risen to great accomplishment from the skills they had obtained.

Some were not suited or inclined to join him in his dreams. They were jealous of their fellows who had. Particularly, two of his slaves were bitter, sought attention and fomented trouble. They were ignorant, wild and reckless.

Daniel and Isaac had taken every advantage of Drish's demeanor and understood Manford's authority was limited. When they were sent unaccompanied to town to pick up supplies, they often listened to the white folks visiting there from the North. The abolitionists incited them with stories about the war and their imminent freedom.

On one visit they heard one who said, "Listen brothers. The Union soldiers are on their way to liberate you from your slaveholder oppressors. Soon you will be free to claim what is yours. There are plans in the government to pay you back for all the labor they have stolen from you. Rise up brothers. The time to defeat them is now."

Isaac looked wild eyed at Daniel and said, "We's needs ta ovathrows them white Mastas now."

Without thinking or realizing that if they would wait just a few days or weeks more, the soldiers would come and resolve it, Isaac too replied, "Let's git that Manford 'n' kill'im."

When Daniel and Isaac got back to Drish plantation, they sought out several of the slaves at the compound of cabins during their personal time after the work day. Daniel didn't know how to plan a revolt, or even how to think it through. He just knew they must overthrow the Massas. There was no plan. They were just angry. They didn't think about their circumstance every day but they did that day.

When Isaac told them, "Them Yankee soldiers is winnin' de war. Purdy soon's they's gonna beat de white devils 'n' we's be free. We's kin fights 'em heah whiles they's weak", one of the group replied, "I heahs 'bout how is on othah plantations. But Drish ain't whips us or takes our families 'way. He ain't paid us fo' ours work, but he's treat us purdy good."

Daniel got angry at this and replied, "Buts we's not free! We's cain't goes 'way whens we wants. We's gots ta kill'em now so's we's be free. That's what's they sayin' in town."

A few in the group went along with them and they staged the revolt.

The revolt they fomented involved nineteen of Drish's slaves, including Daniel and Isaac. They were incensed and fired up to take action and do something. They followed the ill-conceived advice they were given and charged at Manford and his men one morning at the beginning of the work day.

Manford had his three men with him when the slaves came at them. They had shotguns and revolvers like the cavalry had always used for close quarters fighting on horseback. Percussion cap rifled muskets were more suitable for long range use which was deer and wild boar hunting for them.

Their strategy was to keep as much distance as they could against the pitchforks, shovels and wooden axe handles the Negroes were wielding. Those would only work for direct hand-to-hand fighting. The overseers were outnumbered nineteen to four. But they had the advantage of fire power. It would be no contest. All they had to do was not let them get close. The shotguns served as cover fire.

The slaves took whatever cover they could find behind a hay bale or a wagon, even the side of the barn. They did not know how to fight for keeps – for mortality. They acted on instinct only and avoided the shotgun shells this way. The way they figured it, they had only four overseers to kill. But the revolvers got them when they charged senselessly forward.

At this point the yard was clouded with shotgun smoke and pandemonium had broken out. Without thinking, the overseers shot as fast as they could in a panic at anything with black skin.

In the middle of the bloody fracas, Josena was crossing the yard on an errand from the big house. The violence erupted so quickly, she didn't see the danger and couldn't get out of the way in time. She was accidentally shot and killed by one of Manford's men.

When it was over, the ground was pooled with slave's blood. Six of the slaves were killed and eight wounded before they gave up. Two of Manford's men were beaten bloody unconscious but survived. The bodies were scattered over the yard. Josena's body lay there on the ground amongst them in the middle of the yard. It was ghostly quiet when it ended.

When John heard about it moments later, he didn't know what to think. He was stunned and numb – his mind blank at first.

Drish was a physician. He had spent much of his life caring for people. It was rare that he felt or displayed anger toward them.

He had a close relationship with his overseer, John Manford. They did not see eye-to-eye on many things, but there was mutual respect developed over years of working together. Manford was not hesitant to call his boss by his surname and confront him with his opinions. The one thing Manford had to swallow was that he was not allowed to discipline his charges.

After it was over, he said to Manford, "The fools. The bloody fools. I can't feel responsible for the outcome of this stupidity. Now my Josena is gone and Hanna is only eight years old."

Manford looked at him disgusted and replied, "This was bound to happen John. I expected it. I told ya we should have been tougher on them. It's the only thing those animals understand."

It was a shame and an unnecessary tragedy.

In the aftermath, when it was quiet, the bodies were taken away and buried in the cemetery behind the Drish plantation. Sarah was heartbroken when she heard what had happened. She looked at Josena's fresh grave and sadly reflected.

She wondered, 'What will become of Hanna?'

She spoke to John and expressed her concerns, "What are we going to do now?"

"I don't know what to do dear. I thought we were doing a good job of running our lives and theirs."

She said, "I think you should write Ken and Abigail and see if we can bring Hanna to safety."

"That's probably for the best. I'll send him a telegram."

He posted the telegram:

Ken. Coming to meet you on an important matter. Two days. Stop.

Hanna helped Sarah pack up a trunk with all her clothes, dolls and personal keepsakes. Sarah added some personal items of her own so that Hanna would remember her when she got older. She braided Hanna's hair in pigtails with red ribbons, dressed her in the flowered print shift she had made for her, and her white canvas shoes.

The Drishs drove off in their carriage with little Hanna sitting between them. It was a sad and bittersweet trip for them as they headed south to Mobile that sunny morning.

The Union army did come. And they came in force.

In 1865, Lee surrendered to Grant at Appomattox on April 9th.

The cities of Montgomery and Mobile, Alabama surrendered to Union forces on April 12th.

President Lincoln was assassinated in Ford's theater on April 14th.

Confederate General Joe Johnston surrendered to Sherman at Durham Station, NC on April 26th. Like Lee's surrender, Joe Johnston's was cordial and done with honor and mutual respect in keeping with the code they learned at West Point. Both men, and most military leaders on both sides, had more respect and trust in each other than they did for the politicians. The politicians were more suited as their common and natural enemy.

Ironically, so many military leaders followed their war careers in peace time with political office – Grant became President and McClellan tried to run for that office also. All Sherman ever wanted to be was a soldier. The rest of them wanted to go back home and be teachers, farmers, or merchants – whatever they were before – and put it behind them.

Johnston had been fearful his men would be punished for the assassination of Lincoln which had just occurred. He spoke to Sherman of him and said that Lincoln was a man of compassion and forbearance. He felt that if the war ended badly for the Confederacy, Lincoln would have meted out terms that were just and charitable. But now with Lincoln gone, killed by a Confederate sympathizer, he was worried.

Taken with the spirit of their meetings, Sherman offered Johnston terms even more favorable than Grant had done with Lee. He didn't even require that the Rebs abide by Emancipation. Washington - Edwin Stanton - responded angrily to rescind his generosity and General Grant visited Durham Station to retract Sherman's overly generous terms and replace them with a simple agreement as he had done with Lee.

Sherman reflected upon the war after the terms were settled and waxed philosophical about its meaning. He had earlier sent a letter to Confederate General Hardee commiserating about the loss each of them had suffered with the death of their sons. He wrote that now they had both lost their sons at the same time, how unnatural this age is when God's stratagem is violated and the young are unbodied of their souls before the old.

He tried to roughly paraphrase Ecclesiastes when he offered, "As some leaves fall and others grow in their place, so too with the generations of flesh and blood, one dies and another is born."

Grant was solemn also after the cease fires and surrenders because he knew 'Our civil war, the devastating manufacture of the bones of our sons, was but a war after a war, a war before a war'.

Sherman reviewed in his mind the horrific campaign he had waged in the Deep South.

By Christmas of '64, he had destroyed Georgia and occupied Savannah. He had prepared to turn north and continue into the Carolinas. By then he had accumulated a large entourage of freed blacks and displaced whites. Secretary of War Stanton was harshly critical of him for not taking better care of his unwelcome charges. Sherman was livid – ten thousand had been fed and clothed under his orders.

Sherman was deeply resentful of Stanton's visit to Savannah to review his progress and assert his criticisms. He responded with Special Field Order No. 15 just to relieve the political and tactical pressures with the civilian mob that had attached itself to his army. He allocated all the abandoned plantation acreage along the rivers for thirty miles inland in South Carolina, the Sea Islands from Charleston south, parts of Georgia and the country bordering on the St. John's River in Florida for black resettlement. Every free Negro head of a family was given title to forty acres of tillable land, and the seed and equipment to farm their properties.

Sherman was no abolitionist but, in his view, this would shut up Edwin Stanton and disengage the niggers who would stay on their land and plant their forty acres. In those days nearly everyone used that word to describe Africans. For whatever their reasons, that was just how it was.

In Alabama they attacked with infantry and cavalry from the north and naval forces at the port of Mobile in the south. The goal was to capture Montgomery, the first capital of the Confederacy.

Tuscaloosa and surrounding areas in Jefferson and Bibb counties were overrun as Union forces made their final sweeps to destroy any potential military support for the Deep South. The iron furnaces that had forged the metal for John Drish's home had been destroyed as well as the Selma industrial complex.

The abolitionists in town had been correct in their assessment of the situation before the slave revolt. The war had been effectively over for quite some time.

Five- The Old Road South

David decided the answers he was seeking lie in the South. His father and Uncle David had told him all the stories of what happened almost forty years ago. But he needed to see it for himself and see what he could do.

He said to his sister, “Josie, I need to go back there and retrace Father and Uncle David’s personal history.”

Josena could see the troubled look about his face and conviction in his eyes and replied, “I have felt the same way these last few years. I have come to realize the troubles in our country must be solved first in the South.”

“I see it that way too.”

“Let’s go together Dave. We’ve always put our minds together since we were little babies.”

“Ha ha. That is the truth little sister”, he replied with his face shifting to a bright smile.

She pouted and answered, “Listen mister, you are only five minutes older than me.”

Still smiling broadly, David said, “Let’s go tell Father and Mother what we want to do. But we must show them that we have thought it through and have a good plan.”

Josiah and Mary thought that their idea for this trip was a good one. They offered their best horse and carriage for the long journey. They warned them that they would face discrimination in the South with a greater intensity than they had ever experienced in their lives before. They believed that the young ones would likely face danger as well.

Mary told them, "Children, don't think that your clothing, fine carriage and refined speech and appearance will protect you from all white people. There will be some who are ignorant and will look past all that and only see the color of your skin. You will need to know how to handle that."

This consideration led Josena to a greater concern that became a contentious matter for the Ashford family before David and Josena left. She had been thinking about the sociology and the psychology of the people they might encounter and spoke more about it with her mother.

"I agree that our appearance won't protect us, but worse than that, I fear that our refinement of dress and appearance will get us into trouble, Mother."

Mary answered, "It's true you will be traveling through many rural areas like some parts around here, but what do you think you can do about it?"

"I don't know but I don't want to provoke an attack or get robbed. It would be awful if someone stole Father's horse and carriage."

Mary thought it best they have a family meeting to discuss it. The four of them gathered in the dining room to hear Josena's concerns and ideas.

Mary suggested, "I think they would be safer if they don't wear their finest clothing traveling through the South."

Josiah mistook her meaning and angrily replied, “No children of mine are going to pretend they are field niggers to fit in with the locals. What are you suggesting? Do you want them to go in a buckboard work wagon with a plow horse?”

David had been listening to everyone and understood where the conversation was going when he spoke up, “I think Josena is concerned that some of the poor whites might think we are uppity and become provoked. But listen, whether we dress as rich dandies or poor black folk, it won’t make any difference. Either way, if there are jealous blacks or mean-spirited whites, we will have to deal with it.”

Josena came up with the reasoned compromise, “Let’s take your old carriage and leave you your best one here. We will dress properly but modestly, not ostentatiously.”

David was considering the ideas and added, “We can take along our work clothes from the furniture factory in case we need them. The wood stain and ground in wood dust might help our look and come in handy in some circumstances.”

Mary and Josiah worried about their children and feared for them as all parents do. They knew they had to let them go despite the risks. Josie and Dave were grown up, educated, smart and sensible. And, in the end, they knew that this was very important for them. The understanding of the realities of American life could only come from this exploration. They had to have confidence in their children.

Josiah reminded them again the lessons he and David had learned back in those days. They had seen many good and bad people of both races throughout the country. It would be best if they avoided the bad people and the troubles they might bring.

Josiah told them, "Look for the goodness in the people you meet. Form friendship and alliance with them. That will serve you the best and keep you out of danger."

They smiled at the old man's wisdom. They loved him for his care and concern.

Josena responded to his advice, "Thank you Papa. We know you are right. We will follow your advice. You needn't worry. You raised us well."

When Josiah and David Wexley had traveled through the south, they didn't have any maps. They relied on dead reckoning from landmarks and hearsay. But now, when David and Josena were preparing for the trip, Josiah found a map from the 1870's he kept as a memento. So on the day David and Josena Ashford announced they were leaving, with intent to travel south and retrace the route, Josiah offered it to them to bring along.

"Thanks papa, this is a treasure", David said respectfully as he took the old document the day they left.

He and his sister knew it was already badly outdated. But it was interesting to look at it as a piece of history. Much was still the same.

Josiah had marked the route from recollection. Mainly, they had followed the valleys, avoiding the mountain ridges, along the great rivers - the Mississippi, the Tennessee and the Ohio - heading north and then east. The roads were known and well-traveled by pioneers and soldiers before. David and Josie would travel them in reverse.

They left in the spring of 1900 and stayed a couple days in Cincinnati. They had been there before for sightseeing and shopping, but this time they looked up some old college friends who they knew from Oberlin College in Cleveland. They found them there settling their lives in southwestern Ohio, a northern state but with influence of southern climate, culture and values. How different they seemed after years had passed since the youthful college days up in Cleveland.

They were all getting older and the memories of their campus life together were just that - a sweet remembrance. Their classmates were excited to see them. They asked Josie if she was still playing her violin and asked David what he was doing now that he was no longer an academic.

"You two look the same, you down there and him up there", her old girlfriend said. They all laughed.

"What have you been doing Josie? Have you kept up your music?" her friend asked.

She smiled at her friend and said, "I have. We live in Hamilton where you remember we came from. For a few years now I have been running a small music school to teach children violin. Oddly, most of my students are girls. I've learned I enjoy teaching. Soon I plan to go back to college to graduate school and pursue sociology, anthropology, and archeology. That has always been my passion. I haven't married. I have been too busy working at my life.

And David over here, he works at Ashford Furniture Company helping out our father. I expect he will take over one of these days. Our father is getting old."

"That's true Josie", he said. "I also continue my study of history on my own. I have begun writing in my spare time. No wife for me either yet."

They noted together that racial relations were much harsher out in the real world where life happens. That was a shared sadness for them after their youthful idealism had faded.

With their brief reunion over, they crossed the Ohio River and recalled the story of the night Josiah and David had stayed there in Covington, Kentucky – how they had talked through the night looking at the bright lights in Cincinnati. By some inexplicable fortune, they found the same boardinghouse where their father and David had stayed.

The place was over twenty years older and a bit run down and the management wasn't the same. They sat on the same porch one night, more worn than it had been when Josiah and David had sat there.

Josie reflected on the river scene, looked over at Dave and said, "Imagine they were sitting here before they had discovered Hamilton. Before Father had met Mother. Before he had built Ashford Furniture with Uncle David's support. They didn't know then what the future would bring."

David smiled and said, "Just like you and me little sister."

She wrote her father about the place they had found:

7 May, 1900

Dear Papa,
We crossed the Ohio the day before yesterday and stayed in Covington last night. Amazingly, we found the boarding house you told us about. It looks like you described it, maybe a little older.
We looked across the river from the porch and watched the night lights in Cincinnati just as you did.

It was wonderful.

All our Love,
Josie and David

Josie and David followed the old route Josiah and David had followed coming north to Ohio. They rode in their carriage westward in Kentucky along the Ohio River to the Tennessee River and then headed south. There in southwestern Tennessee, they came upon the little hamlet of Shiloh Church.

They knew from the stories they had been told that this was the place where the bloody battle of Pittsburg Landing had been fought.

Josie looked around at the lush landscape, the beautiful manicured fields, the huge weeping willow trees along the river, the quiet pretty hamlet of Shiloh Church and said, "This place is so beautiful. It's nothing like Papa and David described it."

David looked at the long rows and columns of alabaster gravestones, sadly reflected and answered, "Things, places and people change. Without experiencing the history here, we cannot know what it was like then. Imagine that day – the thousands that died so brutally, so fast, the land torn apart from the artillery, the bloody dismembered bodies piled up, the dead quiet when it was over. I can almost see it. But I can never feel it like they did."

"Josie, I've finished reading U.S. Grant's personal memoirs. It was published in 1885 just before he died. He wrote in two volumes about his whole life as a boy, a soldier and a president. He said in the preface that 'Man proposes and God disposes'. At the end of the first volume he wrote about this place and the battle of Pittsburg Landing.

He commanded the Army of the Ohio here and was reinforced by Buell nearby in Corinth. They fought against the collected army of Johnston. Sherman supported with his Army of the Tennessee. On Friday, April 4th, he was injured by his horse falling with him while trying to get to the front.

But he had deep sympathy and understanding for everyone who fought here and died or survived. He dedicated his book to the commanders and soldiers of both the National and Confederate governments."

Josie wondered, 'What must it have been like then for Uncle David coming to see it'?

She looked at the vast flat green space populated so full of the white death stones in an almost endless, perfect geometric grid.

"David, when they were here it was the aftermath of the carnage. The ground was still torn up and scorched from that day. But the bodies had been collected and buried. There were so many at once they couldn't do it with care. They just wrapped them in white cloth, piled them into large pits and poured lime on the ground before they covered them up. I don't know how they could sort it out later to identify anyone to rebury them proper."

David replied, "They didn't. The markers are just ceremonial. The names were known from the records of the soldiers that had been killed or missing. Their bodies are still under there with their comrades-in-arms piled together. They never had time or inclination to place grave markers. I read that whenever they knew the man's name, they wrote it on a scrap of paper, put it in a bottle and tucked it under the blouse of his tunic."

"They were so young, our age or most of them even younger", Josie reflected.

"I know it. This was the place where they gave the last full measure of devotion, like President Lincoln had said. That's why these places are hallowed ground", David answered.

"Papa understood this. He was here with Uncle."

David smiled at her knowingly and said, "Papa knew that both sides had given their last full measure of devotion for their cause. He learned that here. That's why he came to care about all the American people when he began his political career."

"But how could he forgive them for slavery?"

"I don't know for certain. But his faith brought him to forgive so he could live his life in peace without hate consuming him. Our father is a very special and great man."

Josie looked seriously at David and said, "I know he is. We are blessed to have him."

She wrote her father:

14 May, 1900

Dearest Papa,

We stopped today at Pittsburg Landing to visit the site of the battle of Shiloh as you and David Wexley had done so many years ago. It is a national monument now for its important role in our history.

I'm sure it looks different than when you were here. It is green and lush and pretty, but of course somber as well. The grass is manicured and the lime from the mass graves must have leached out of the soil and diluted by now.

David said this battle had been misunderstood at the time. Grant was here and commanded his forces from a gunboat on the Tennessee, stepping off to the landing to get a closer look at his forces. Lee was back east and not involved.

This battle was more monumental than Manassas or Wilson's Creek, but the public didn't know the scope of it or the size of the forces aligned there or the number of losses that occurred. So many men died there for their own two causes.

We could see in our mind's eye Grant looking up the bluff from the landing, the men assembled on the field above – Grant's General Sherman facing the Confederate attack from Johnston's Army of the Mississippi led by Beauregard's Generals Bragg, Polk, Breckinridge and Hardee.

Twenty four thousand men died here in two days. It is heartbreaking to remember that. Thank God the Union was preserved and our people emancipated. But what an immense price to pay. No one expected that.

Be well. We will keep in contact as we go along.

Love and Respect Always,
Josie and David

They left Pittsburgh Landing and headed down the Tennessee to Alabama, next to the border of Mississippi. The plan was to find the Drish Plantation in Tuscaloosa.

David said, "We'll have to head south and stay in Alabama. Tuscaloosa is almost due south of here. It's almost half way down the western side of the state going toward Mobile at the Gulf of Mexico."

"Yessir big brother. No more big rivers for a while. The Mississippi River is way west of here on her western border."

Josie was thinking about the Mississippi River as an important part of the South and said to David, "You know Dave there is a literary South. That is, there is a lot that has been written about it. Harriet Beecher Stowe made a powerful case for ending slavery in *Uncle Tom's Cabin*, Samuel Clemens from Missouri has been writing about the Mississippi for years now. He worked as a riverboat pilot there and chose his pen name, Mark Twain, because of the term the men used to call out the river depth of two fathoms, twelve feet, which was a safe depth for steamboat navigation.

Those literary Souths tell us some more about the history you have studied. They are intellectual and poetic and describe the landscape as well as the people. The land has always been important to the southerners. The writers describe the landscape, including the seascape, and the sky with the eye of the artist. So often it is about the light – the sunrises, sunsets and vast panorama of stars in the night.

They write about the southern angst of guilt and inferiority – apology for lack of refinement and the deep sins past. They write about glory, chivalry, gentility and courtliness, maybe sewn from an older European past. They write about the human condition and the old verities of good and evil, love and hate, cruelty, kindness and faith."

David agreed, "I know that's true. You're the humanities woman."

He launched into a big lecture on the South, "But there are at least five geographical Souths – maybe more.

There is the South along the Atlantic coast, maybe starting from Annapolis, Maryland near where Uncle David came from, and going all the way to the Spanish South in Florida. All along this coast there are diverse geographies. In the Upper South, it is the Chesapeake Bay, the Potomac River and the Shenandoah Valley. Along the coast there are the ocean ports of Norfolk, Virginia and Charleston, South Carolina and the river access ports at Savannah, Georgia and Saint Augustine, Florida. Along South Carolina and Georgia there is the low country with its sentimental tidewaters and its mysterious sea islands.

There is the Creole South and the Gulf South of Louisiana and the southern shores of Alabama and Mississippi, the panhandle of Florida and even the Gulf coast of Texas. It's so different there – French and Catholic. The Africans there were freed before the Civil War. There is a strong Caribbean flavor, so different than what we know about.

There is the Mississippi River South, the line where the river waterway bisects the continent from north to south and extends from the heartland to join with the Missouri in St. Louis, continues through Tennessee, passes along the border of Arkansas, to its delta in Louisiana where it terminates in the Gulf of Mexico.

There is the Appalachian Mountain South, with the Blue Ridge, the Ozark and the Allegheny in North Carolina, West Virginia and Arkansas.

There is the rural South in the remote and desolate inland backroads of southwest Georgia, Alabama and Mississippi.

All of these are bound together with a similar, if regionally unique, culture spread over a vast region of America.

We northerners can't ignore how big and important it is."

Josie looked at him and said, "I guess so. There's more there than I realized. Thanks for that geography lesson. I know it's a big and diverse region of our country. I think about it as just three vast regions – the northern South, the southern South and the western South."

"I see what you mean. That does encapsulate it quite simply."

As they continued south from Tennessee into Alabama, they realized the great river meandered to the east. They broke away and turned south toward the Muscle Shoals area where Andrew Jackson had fought the Cherokee peoples. Their Chickamauga faction had moved south from there and settled along the Chickamauga River. David and Josie followed their old trail. It was rural and they didn't encounter any cities or any sign of modern civilization.

They got lost on a dirt back road in a remote wooded area. David spotted an old cabin next to a small farm and they headed up the entrance road. Before they got too close, an old man came out of the cabin with his shotgun pointed at them. It wasn't pointed at them exactly. Both barrels were loaded with fresh shells and it was broken open laying over the crook of his left arm – friendly but cautious.

"Where do ya' think your goin' niggers?" he asked.

Josie was annoyed and started to rebuff him, "Who the hell do you ..."

David cut her off quick, "Hush up your mouth woman. I'll speak to this gentleman".

He calmly answered, "Don't mean no trouble mister. We got lost back up the road".

"You looks like uppity northern niggers to me. What you doin' in these parts?"

David continued, "We're just tryin' to find the main road to Tuscaloosa. If you would be kind enough to tell us, we'll be on our way".

"It's back up the road ya jus' come two miles. Ya missed the turn."

Josie finally smartened up and said, "Thank you kindly sir. We be right otta your way."

"Good then, stay offa my property and good riddance to ya."

South of Lake Tuscaloosa, they found the city. There they found the imprint and remnants of John Drish that had dominated Tuscaloosa's early development and recovery after the war. The college had been rebuilt and revived. But John and Sarah were long gone and buried thirty one and fourteen years before.

They found his house but Josie said, "I think we need to talk to the people at the University of Alabama and find out what happened here."

David smiled and offered, "Thinking like the academic you are little sister."

"Of course, and you can stop that little sister nonsense any time you like. We're both thirty one years old", she snapped.

"Sorry Josie. You are right. Let's go talk to the local historians at the university."

“We’re tired from a long day of travel. Let’s get something to eat and a good night’s sleep before we do that.”

Six – Redeeming Hanna

After breakfast the next morning, they found the history department at the university.

Professor McPherson told them, "I remember John and Sarah well. They were good people."

"But they were slaveholders, Professor", Josie offered.

"Yes they were. But they were different than most around here. They treated their people very well - like family. You sound like northern coloreds. You don't know how it was for everyone here in the South."

David could see that Josena was about to enter into another argument. He knew it was more important to find out what they could about their father's daughter than win the debate.

Annoyed, he changed the tone of the conversation, "The Drishs had a female slave named Josena there before the war. We heard she had a daughter on the Drish Plantation before she died. We are trying to find the daughter."

"What for?" he asked.

Josie answered, "Because she is our sister. Our father, Josiah Ashford, was married to the slave girl, Josena".

The Professor offered, "All I can tell you is that it was very confusing at that time. The Union was at our door ready to demolish our city. The Drishs left and I guess they took the girl with them. When they came back after we were overrun, she wasn't with them."

David looked crestfallen and said, "That's it then? No one knows where she disappeared to?"

"I have an idea though. It's just a guess", the Professor offered. "They had some good friends, the Blanchards who live in Mobile. Maybe they took her there. Do you know how to find Mobile?"

Josie smirked, "Thanks. I think we can manage."

"Thanks for the help, Professor. We'll be on our way there", David concurred.

The areas south of Tuscaloosa became more populated as they headed toward the great port of Mobile on the Mobile Bay. They knew they were getting close to the Gulf of Mexico when they began to smell the salty air.

The Blanchards were easy to find. They were a prominent family with a prosperous well-known business. Their beautiful city estate was a wonder to see. David and Josena felt more comfortable in this more "civilized" location.

As they walked up the sidewalk to the Blanchards' beautiful red brick mansion on the morning they came to call, Josie said, "I wonder what they will be like, David."

"I wonder if she is here."

A servant answered their knock at the front door.

"We are here to see the Blanchards", David announced.

The butler was guarded and suspicious of the colored strangers appearing at the front door. He had his rules to follow.

"I'se sorry folks, niggers has ta go to the back do'", the butler told them.

Josie thought, 'I don't have to bow or scape. I am entitled to my dignity. I must maintain my integrity. I am supposed to kill them with kindness, but I am not my father. And this is not the white man, but his person.'

She paused a long moment staring at him, trying to think what to do and at last said, "Go back in that house and tell your master the Ashfords from Ohio are here on an important family matter and need to speak to him. We will wait for you here."

The butler stood there looking at them, their refined appearance, their educated manner, their comportment, and wasn't sure what to do. He was colored like them, but they were different. These folks weren't holding their hats in their hands figuratively or literally.

They tried to explain their purpose. The butler was still uncertain what to do. But he became more relaxed and decided to go speak to his master. He smiled at them and asked them to wait while he conferred with Ken Blanchard.

When he came back to the door, he invited them in to wait in the grand foyer. It was spacious, cool and dark and adorned with Italian marble floors and columns.

He said, "Please wait here. I'll git Mista Blanchard to come speak to ya."

Ken came along to the foyer in his dressing gown and leather slippers. But he looked dressed up with his white silk shirt and scarf under his formal morning wear. Abigail trailed along right behind him to see who had come to visit. She was dressed for the day and looked like she might have an important engagement planned for later.

David started the conversation, "Mister Blanchard, thank you for receiving us so early in the day. We are on an important mission and need to speak to you if you are agreeable."

Ken saw that they were a fine young well dressed and well-spoken colored couple and was curious what they were about.

"It's all my pleasure son. I'm interested in what your mission might be. We don't get to talk to many young folks anymore. This is my Missus, Abigail and you can call me Ken.

We have finished our breakfast, but would love to have our coffee and have you join us. If you haven't eaten, our cook will want you to have your most important meal of the day."

Josie smiled, said, "Most kind of you Mister Blanchard. I am Josena Ashford and this is David Ashford."

"You're a handsome couple and it's good to meet you", Abigail chimed in.

David laughed, "We are brother and sister. She is my twin."

Wondering where they were from, Abigail asked, "Have you traveled far to come to Mobile, Josena?"

Josie nodded and said, "Yes. We live in Hamilton, Ohio. That's just a bit north of Cincinnati. It has been a long trip."

It suddenly occurred to Abigail that the young woman's name was familiar and maybe a coincidence.

"Oh my. We raised a little colored girl here years ago. Her mother was killed and her mother's name was Josena. It's an unusual name", she said.

Josie gasped, "My Lord in Heaven. Wait until we tell you our story. That little girl you raised may be our older sister."

"Pray tell Josena. I need to hear this story", Abigail said.

They joined the Blanchards for breakfast and spent all of the morning telling each other their stories.

Finally Ken told them, "The little girl we raised here was named Hanna – Hanna Drish. John and Sarah had named her when she was born on their plantation. They truly loved her as a daughter. They had no children of their own. It was heartbreaking for them to bring her here and give her up.

Of course that was years ago when Hanna was eight and the war was ending. She's a grown woman now, older than you. She left in '82 and let me see – she must be about forty four now."

David anxiously asked, "Why did she leave and where did she go?"

"Hanna is a very unusual woman with a spiritual mission. She received a calling to go west and seek her solutions. We have not seen or heard from her in many years. We just know she was heading west, probably into Mississippi", Abigail replied.

They exchanged departing pleasantries and thanked the Blanchards for their kind help.

As they walked down the street to their carriage, Josie opined, "Well now we have lost the trail, David. What are we going to do?"

"I think we should just head west and look for Father's old plantation – Savannah Oaks."

They wrote home again:

28 May, 1900

Dearest Mother and Father,
Josie and I are leaving Mobile, Alabama heading for Mississippi. We met the Blanchards, a white couple, who raised our sister here in their home. Ken Blanchard told us her name is Hanna Drish.
She was named after the Drish family at the plantation you and David Wexley found. When we were there in Tuscaloosa, we learned the Drishs were dead. A professor at the college thought she might have been taken to their friends, the Blanchards at the end of the war.
But for now we have lost the trail for her whereabouts - we just know she went west. We will head that way too and look for your old plantation over near Natchez.
Be well. We will write you again soon.

Love Always,
David and Josena

They didn't want to get their father's hopes too high or theirs either. And so they continued, not sure what they would find or learn next.

Traveling west by horse and carriage, they traversed the little bit of Alabama quickly and soon came to the border of Mississippi. Near Biloxi, they regrouped and had a talk.

"You know Mobile was once part of Mississippi, David?"

"Yes, I knew that it was captured and added to the Mississippi Territory in 1813. Then it became part of the Alabama Territory in 1817."

"Well anyway, since we are headed toward Natchez, I know we have to swing north at some point. I was thinkin' we might stay along the Gulf Coast for a ways. We'll come to New Orleans. What do you think, Dave?'

"It might be fun and interesting, but I really want to get to our destination and find Savannah Oaks plantation."

"Well then we can cut across a corner of Louisiana as we head northwest toward Natchez. I am really interested in the Louisiana people from a sociology standpoint. We studied the Creole culture, the French influences and the African Voodoo pseudo-religious beliefs in my old classes."

"That's interesting Josie. I remember too that many of the slaves there were freedmen long before the war. Let's do that."

"Sadly, some of them had businesses and held slaves themselves. What a cruel sellout to our own people, David."

After a brief stay in New Orleans, they passed through some remote areas in northeast Louisiana and did meet some of the people there – all poor black and white farmers. The topography and the people didn't change much as they crossed the border again back into Mississippi.

David and Josena remembered their father telling them that Savannah Oaks was about sixty miles west of Natchez on the Mississippi.

"We'll need to aim for Natchez", he told her.

They rode across Mississippi from its southeast to its central west. It was all much the same – a country with no big cities, small towns, rural areas, simple mostly friendly white and black folks, a few living together, most living, working and worshipping apart, the same country culture with white folks and black folks going into and out of their churches on the Sabbath, worshipping their same God, together in large extended family outdoor gatherings to share food and fellowship, playing music on banjos, washboards and fiddles, singing and dancing, loving their families, tilling the same soil, loving and respecting their freedom and independence – in the South.

After many days, they came to the small town of McComb, Mississippi. David knew they were close to the old plantation, Savannah Oaks. The locals explained to them that the town was formerly part of the plantation and directed them out the old road to the mansion nearby – still standing.

As they approached the old plantation on the entrance road, the long unattended branches from the live oaks hung down so low that the gray Spanish moss brushed their faces as their carriage pushed through.

When they arrived at the circle in front of the majestic mansion, Josie said, "Let's look inside."

David pushed the overgrowth away from the entrance and they entered into the cavernous, dark, cool and musty foyer. Nature had reclaimed her grounds and the mold, mildew, weather, insects and pests had wreaked their havoc on her insides. Forty years of abandonment had surely taken its toll.

From years of neglect, the paint on the ceilings had mostly peeled away and hung down in stained strips revealing the tarnished sheet metal underneath. The tapestries on the walls were black with mold from the years of shaded dampness.

Damage to the roof had let years of rain pour into the grand rooms on the second floor. All throughout the house, the floors were covered with debris and small creatures scurried away as they approached. Most of the furniture was gone, had been stolen by the Yankees and the remaining after by the locals.

David looked at Josie and said, "This must have been a great place of grandeur for the white folks here once."

"Yes, and their colored slaves must have served their every need in their grand way of life", she sarcastically added.

As they continued to explore through the wreckage, they came to the huge kitchen in the back. The large pecan table, covered with dirt, still stood solidly in its place.

"I remember Father telling us he built this when he worked here as a carpenter and woodworker. He was proud of it", Josie recalled.

David thought and said, "This was maybe the first great piece of Ashford furniture ever made."

After a while, their reconnoitering became too painful and they decided to leave. In the bright sunshine in the yard they passed by the whipping post, not knowing what it was or what had happened there. But God knew and He remembered.

"I must see the slave cabins", Josie told him.

The cabins in the long row were dilapidated – their roofs mostly caved in and their walls leaning over, long out of square and plumb. They entered one of the small rough buildings and saw the years of feces pellets and urine stains from the mice and the squirrels that had infested the torn covers of the cotton stuffed mattress on the small bed. There was broken glass scattered on the small table from the smashed oil lantern still sitting there.

"This is where Father lived as a young slave", David imagined.

They followed the narrow dirt path to the top of the hill and found an open-sided building with a collapsed roof covered with dirt and leaves.

David noticed the rusty machinery underneath and remarked to Josie, "This must have been the saw mill where Papa milled the wood for the plantation".

With heavy hearts, they looked back as they left the plantation and drove their carriage back to town. They were worn out and needed rest.

"I am so despondent David", she told him.

"Me as well Josie", he said.

"I'm going to write father and at least tell him we saw Savannah Oaks", she said.

"That's probably a good idea until we figure out what to do now. Don't sadden him though. Try to keep it kind to his heart."

"I will", she said and wrote him:

12 June, 1990

Dear Father,

We found Savannah Oaks today and saw where you lived and worked. The place is abandoned and run down now which probably doesn't surprise you. We even saw the cabins you lived in and your old sawmill.

Raised in the north long after emancipation as freeborn people, it was quite an experience for us. You were so strong and brave and suffered so much to get where you are today.

All our love and enduring respect,
Josie and David

They stayed in town with a colored family who took them in as boarders. The way that came about was circuitous and disconcerting. There they put aside their conflicted melancholy feelings about the plantation and thought about their sister. They found an old colored woman walking on the street and stopped to speak to her.

Josie asked her, "Have you heard about a black woman that might have come here from Mississippi years ago?"

The colored woman thought and spoke, "They's a wuman like dat. We don't gets many stangahs comin' heah so I'se 'membahs ha comin'."

"Who was she?" David asked.

"She a healah in these heah parts. She live wid dat ole witch, Nora Travers down suth ovs town in da swamp forest."

"What is her name? Do you know?" asked Josie.

"Course I does. Evrabody know ha. She Hanna Drish".

They were astounded. They had found their sister.

Seven – The Klu Klux Klan

Shortly after the conclusion of the war, retired Confederate General Nathan Bedford Forrest participated in the emerging KKK. He was embittered about the loss of the war. His motive was to preserve the American traditional way of life as he viewed it as a southerner. Later, his son William's son, Nathan Bedford Forest II, from Oxford Mississippi became the Grand Dragon of the KKK.

They knew the southern way of life was changing and the lost cause could not be won back. Some southerners thought the next best thing they could do was to take the law into their own hands, for their own purpose. Many white men in the South saw it that way.

It would be a great mission of intimidation, of dominance, of retribution and punishment. It would be a lesson to all of white superiority over Negroes, Jews and Catholics – all the peoples that didn't belong, or shouldn't belong, and had no rightful place in the purity of American society.

Their means was to organize a group of like-thinking men. They would disguise themselves in white robes and hoods and ride on horseback into the night as an army of reformers to terrorize the black freedmen and their white sympathizers.

They would hold ceremonies and secretly celebrate their cause on the hillsides. They would shoot and kill Negroes who they viewed as a threat. They would burn them out of their houses and hang them with rope nooses from trees until they were dead. They would burn crosses on their front lawns to terrorize them and strike fear into their hearts. This scourge of society would be a lesson and a way to strike back for the injustice suffered by the Confederacy.

Why wouldn't God intervene and stop this cruelty and inhumanity by some white men against their fellow man that they viewed as inferior? Now that He was old, He didn't seem to care and strike them down. But surely He had been young once and had brought His wrath upon man when He knew they had gone too far.

Maybe, because He was old now, He had seen too much of His children's hate for one another and decided they must resolve it for themselves. He still had the power to solve it, but was tired and disappointed in His creation. He had given them free will and He knew the price of that.

He watched and He waited and He hoped. He knew that His Angels had enlisted humans like Hanna to work as His instrument.

In a simply amazing turnabout and change of heart, the old General met with black southerners in 1875 at a meeting of their organization, the Independent Order of the Pole-Bearers Association, when he declared to them in his speech the following:

Ladies and Gentlemen I accept the flowers as a memento of reconciliation between the white and colored races of the southern states. I accept it more particularly as it comes from a colored lady, for if there is any one on God's earth who loves the ladies I believe it is myself.

This day is a day that is proud to me, having occupied the position that I did for the past twelve years, and been misunderstood by your race. This is the first opportunity I have had during that time to say that I am your friend. I am here a representative of the southern people, one more slandered and maligned than any man in the nation.

I will say to you and to the colored race that men who bore arms and followed the flag of the Confederacy are, with very few exceptions, your friends. I have an opportunity of saying what I have always felt – that I am your friend, for my interests are your interests, and your interests are my interests. We were born on the same soil, breathe the same air, and live in the same land. Why, then, can we not live as brothers? I will say that when the war broke out I felt it my duty to stand by my people. When the time came I did the best I could, and I don't believe I flickered. I came here with the jeers of some white people, who think that I am doing wrong. I believe that I can exert some influence, and do much to assist the people in strengthening fraternal relations, and shall do all in my power to bring about peace. It has always been my motto to elevate every man- to depress none. I want to elevate you to take positions in law offices, in stores, on farms, and wherever you are capable of going.

I have not said anything about politics today. I don't propose to say anything about politics. You have a right to elect whom you please; vote for the man you think best, and I think, when that is done, that you and I are freemen. Do as you consider right and honest in electing men for office. I did not come here to make you a long speech, although invited to do so by you. I am not much of a speaker, and my business prevented me from preparing myself. I came to meet you as friends, and welcome you to the white people. I want you to come nearer to us. When I can serve you I will do so. We have but one flag, one country; let us stand together. We may differ in color, but not in sentiment. Use your best judgement in selecting men for office and vote as you think right.

Many things have been said about me which are wrong, and which white and black persons here, who stood by me through the war, can contradict. I have been in the heat of battle when colored men, asked me to protect them. I have placed myself between them and the bullets of my men, and told them they should be kept unharmed. Go to work, be industrious, live honestly and act truly, and when you are oppressed I'll come to your relief. I thank you, ladies and gentlemen, for this opportunity you have afforded me to be with you, and to assure you that I am with you in heart and in hand.

His kind words and ovations to the colored people were well received.

But when God heard this, He was more skeptical. He remembered that just seventy years ago Thomas Jefferson had made the same kind, friendly offerings to the Native American nation in 1806. He spoke to them in person, just as Forrest had done here to the colored people. Behind their backs, President Jefferson had told William H. Harrison, his governor of Indian Territory that we must live in perpetual peace with the Indians, but if they did not incorporate as cooperative American citizens with the many white settlers moving into their areas, they must be pushed out of the way and removed beyond the Mississippi.

Forrest's farewell address to his troops at Gainesville, Alabama on May 9, 1865 is also revealing of his heart and character:

Civil war, such as you have just passed through naturally engenders feelings of animosity, hatred, and revenge. It is our duty to divest ourselves of all such feelings; and as far as it is in our power to do so, to cultivate friendly feelings towards those with whom we have so long contended, and heretofore so widely, but honestly, differed. Neighborhood feuds, personal animosities, and private differences should be blotted out; and, when you return home, a manly, straightforward course of conduct will secure the respect of your enemies. Whatever your responsibilities may be to Government, to society, or to individuals meet them like men.

The attempt made to establish a separate and independent Confederation has failed; but the consciousness of having done your duty faithfully, and to the end, will, in some measure, repay for the hardships you have undergone. In bidding you farewell, rest assured that you carry with you my best wishes for your future welfare and happiness. Without, in any way, referring to the merits of the Cause in which we have been engaged, your courage and determination, as exhibited on many hard-fought fields, has elicited the respect and admiration of friend and foe. And I now cheerfully and gratefully acknowledge my indebtedness to the officers and men of my command whose zeal, fidelity and unflinching bravery have been the great source of my past success in arms.

I have never, on the field of battle, sent you where I was unwilling to go myself; nor would I now advise you to a course which I felt myself unwilling to pursue. You have been good soldiers, you can be good citizens. Obey the laws, preserve your honor, and the Government to which you have surrendered can afford to be, and will be, magnanimous.

Nathan Bedford Forrest was revered by his men for his spirit, his boldness and his leadership. Like his fellow flamboyant Confederate cavalry general, Jeb Stuart, they loved him and held him with deep affection.

Confederate General Bragg had sent him north over the Tennessee River, deep into enemy territory, where he was surrounded on all sides and placed himself in a tight spot.

General Forrest led his cavalry on surprise raids and ruined the Union's strategic railroads, captured hundreds of their soldiers and their supplies desperately needed by the Confederacy. He escaped their traps brilliantly and with some good fortune. His efforts delayed General Grant's eventual victory at Vicksburg and the ultimate Union control of the Mississippi.

He was admired also by the other Confederate leaders and feared by those of the Union. It was a shame after the war for himself, and about himself, that he turned his passion for his country to such a bitterness toward its newly freed African citizens.

Nathan Bedford Forrest, like much of the southern country, had turned his sorrow for the lost cause to a dark place of hatred – racism. But that is what he did, the man he became, and he shall forever be remembered in infamy.

He had lent his good name to the cause of the KKK and that solidified his reputation in history. A man has to be considered for all his life's deeds and hypocrisies. Only God can judge him.

Hanna knew of the KKK's presence. Their actions were known to all people of the South. They all had seen them or, at the least, heard the stories about them. She couldn't just ignore them or, even as a Christian woman, forgive them. But God had warned her of evil.

She chose to follow her own path. She knew her best way to serve her God was to subvert them by her example, as she had learned in the bible, by mustering the forces of good white people and good black people working together. This would allow her to keep her promise and offset the evil hatred of the KKK.

She would leave the vengeance to Him. She knew from Ezekiel 25:17, God had said:

> *And I will execute great vengeance upon them with wrathful rebukes; and they shall know that I am Jehovah, when I shall lay my vengeance upon them.*

Hanna had nothing to fear. She had felt the spirit and had read the book, knew the Revelation, and how it would end for mankind. She has seen the Alpha and the Omega and understood the meaning of the beginning and the end. The Lord had told her there will be a day of reckoning when He would return and we will all pay for our sins.

All her life He had told her what that will mean for us here – here in our time and our country. But she knew the time was drawing near when we would pay for our sins. Our chance for salvation as a nation under God was slipping away.

Someday the old God of Abraham would return with a vengeance because man had failed to follow His Lamb Jesus. Those that did not repent would be smote to ashes by His might.

The KKK was not her worry. All she had to do was act justly, love mercy, and walk humbly with her God.

But she remembered something Ken Blanchard had told her back in Mobile when she was younger. He had helped her understand the important difference between two words – empathy and sympathy.

He had explained that empathy was a feeling we could have for people who are different. It meant we could not understand them very well because they are different, but we could walk a mile in their shoes to understand them better.

Sympathy is a feeling, he explained, we can only have for people who are the same as we are. But if we practice empathy long enough and far enough, we can become more the same. When that happens, we can begin to have the rarer feeling of sympathy.

Hanna realized this understanding and practice would help her keep her promise. She followed it more and more as she became older and wiser.

Eight - Tuscaloosa

Shortly after the slave revolt, and with Josena fresh in her grave, the Yankees came to Tuscaloosa. Within sight of the Union forces at their gates, John and Sarah were horrified and fled for their lives. Their concern was more for Hanna than themselves.

They knew that Mobile was occupied by the Yankees – had been for some time. From regular communication, they knew that Ken and Abigail were safe there. They were hemmed in but safe, the conditions more quiet and stable. The Yankees did not destroy their infrastructure since they needed the port for their purposes.

John hated to leave. He was panicked and feared they would burn his house down in his absence. If that was to be their intent, they would burn it down in his presence anyway. So they decided to leave for Hanna's sake, and left their property in the hands of fate and their people.

Their house was spared. But the University of Alabama wasn't. Almost all of the buildings on the new campus were burned and nearly destroyed.

It wasn't a siege like in Vicksburg or Atlanta. With little defense, Tuscaloosa was merely overrun in short order. There were fires spread all over the small city. John was gone by then and didn't see it. His beautiful home was mostly masonry and iron, so it wasn't worth the extra trouble to put it to the torch. Most of its contents were looted. Whether they deserved it or not would be up to God to decide.

Union Brigadier General James H. Wilson was under orders from and served under Grant in the Western Theater. Wilson came from Illinois and died in Delaware long after the war.

He had defeated Nathan Bedford Forrest in the Battle of Franklin and again during his raid through Alabama in what was called Wilson's Raid. He sent 1500 men under John T. Croxton to burn the Roupes Valley Ironworks and Bibb Naval Furnace at Brierfield and the University of Alabama at Tuscaloosa where a prominent military school was attached. Cadets from there graduated to serve as officers in the Confederate army.

When the college was burned on April 4, 1865, it was only five days before Lee's surrender at Appomattox. Only four buildings survived the fires. In retrospect, the destruction appeared unnecessary.

John changed after the war. That is, he made changes to accommodate the new reality. He was forced to by the circumstances, but it was for the better. He was the same man but became more so. He never liked the system of slavery anyway. The changes made him happier.

He remembered his overseer, John Manford and thought, 'He managed things for me well enough but when he was gut shot and killed by that freed slave and Yankee soldier after the revolt and Josena's death, I knew it was time for things to be done different. They had had an altercation with Manford and stole two of my best horses when they shot him and fled that day. I'd had enough of the plantation way of the South by the end of the war anyway. Emancipation of the slaves was long overdue.'

His interest in growing cotton had always been secondary, so he parceled off most of his land. The new schemes of share cropping and tenant farming held no appeal for him because he could see that these solutions kept the farmers in another form of economic bondage.

Most plantation owners, after releasing their slaves, had kept their land as the last asset of value that remained for them. John had a better vision, so he sold off his land to small independent farmers - freedmen and whites – who bought it outright. John helped them finance it and held their mortgages.

The Drishs concentrated on their strongest enterprises – the cotton ginning services and mechanical repair services and sales of equipment in support of the independent cotton producers.

The growing city of Tuscaloosa bought 100 acres of his land to facilitate their recovery and expansion. John and Sarah invested in rebuilding the University of Alabama that was destroyed there during the war. With the urbanization of Tuscaloosa, Drish plantation became Drish estate and blended into the city. His beautiful home was now located on 2300 17th Street.

But Sarah and John were lonely. It was too quiet on their estate now. They missed Hanna but knew she was doing well with Ken and Abigail in Mobile.

Alabama's history was closely related to and derived from Mississippi's. John was there in Tuscaloosa for many of Alabama's transitions throughout its evolution. He witnessed and lived through it but with his gentler Virginia sensibilities. He most often followed his own path apart from the regional culture.

He told Sarah on many occasions, "My dear, I don't see the benefit of slavery to anybody in our country, our state or our city. I know it will end because it must."

She loved him for that and agreed, "Ultimately God will punish us and the South for our sins and transgressions. We have gone against nature and Him and will be punished for it in the end."

Prior to the admission of Mississippi as a state in 1817, the sparsely populated eastern half of the territory was named the Alabama Territory. It had been created by the U.S. Congress later that year.

The former town of St. Stephens was the territorial capital until 1819. Then Congress selected Huntsville as the site for the first Constitutional Convention of Alabama after it was approved to become the 22nd state. Delegates met to prepare the new state's constitution. Huntsville served as the temporary capital of Alabama until 1820.

Alabama fever was well underway when the state was admitted to the Union. Settlers and speculators poured into the area to take advantage of fertile land for cotton cultivation. It was part of the frontier in the 1820s and 1830s with a constitution providing white men suffrage.

Like John Drish, southeastern planters and traders from the upper South brought slaves with them as the cotton plantations expanded. The economy of this central Black Belt, named for its dark soil, was built around the large plantations. The owners grew wealthy from their slave labor.

Alabama also drew many poor white people who became the disenfranchised subsistence farmers. By 1810, the population was still under 10,000 but increased to more than 300,000 by 1830 after John came in 1822. Native American tribes were removed from there shortly after the Congress passed the Indian Removal Act in 1830.

From 1826 to 1846, Tuscaloosa was Alabama's capital, until Montgomery became the capital after that. Its former capital building, built in 1827-1829, was designed by a man named William Nichols, a friend of John Drish, who shared his passion for architecture.

In 1846, the Alabama legislature voted to move the capital city from Tuscaloosa to Montgomery. A new capital building was erected there under the direction of Stephen Decatur Button of Philadelphia. Barachias Holt of Exeter, Maine designed it. It was burned down in 1849 and rebuilt in 1851.

By 1860, Alabama's population had increased to nearly one million people. Nearly half were enslaved African Americans. A small number of free people of color lived there along with them. When Alabama seceded from the Union, it joined the Confederacy just a few days after being an independent republic. Montgomery was the capital of the Confederacy at that time.

Nathan Bedford Forrest's battalion from Kentucky were joined by cavalry solders from Huntsville, Alabama. Their company wore yellow trim on the sleeves, collar and coat tails of their uniform to distinguish themselves. Hence they were greeted as Yellowhammer which later became the nickname for all of Alabama's Confederate troops.

Officially Alabama's slaves were freed by the 13th Amendment in 1865. The state was under military rule from the end of the war in May 1865 until its official restoration to the Union in 1868.

From 1867 to 1874, most white citizens were temporarily barred from voting, while freedmen were enfranchised. Thus, many African Americans emerged as political leaders in the state and were represented in Congress.

Following the war, the state remained chiefly agricultural, with an economy tied to cotton. As part of their share of, and requirement of, reconstruction, the state legislators ratified a new state constitution in 1868, creating the first public schools and expansion of women's rights. Public projects for roads and railroads were hampered by allegations of fraud and misappropriations.

Organized insurgent groups arose to win back the lost cause of the Confederacy and the southern way of life. These resistance groups called themselves redeemers, but were predatory raiders who fomented violence in an already deeply devastated part of America. The original Klu Klux Klan was short lived but other groups like the Knights of the White Camellia, Red Shirts and the White League carried the banner of southern honor.

Reconstruction in Alabama ended in 1874, when the Democrats regained control of the legislature and governor's office through an election dominated by fraud and violence. They wrote another constitution in 1875, and the legislature passed the Blaine Amendment, prohibiting public money from being used to finance religious-affiliated schools.

That same year, legislation was approved that called for racially segregated schools. Railroad passenger cars were segregated in 1891. After disfranchising most African Americans and many poor whites in the 1901 constitution, the Alabama legislature passed more Jim Crow laws at the beginning of the 20th century to impose segregation in everyday life.

John lived through the war and its immediate aftermath until his accidental death in 1867. Sarah lived through the brunt of all that and the many changes that followed. She remained there in Tuscaloosa for almost all of it until her death in 1884. She lived alone as a widow grieving for her husband nearly twenty years after his tragic premature death.

The Drishs were largely responsible for the growth and development of the city. Their family name remained prominent throughout most of its history and was memorialized after their passing. They left no heirs and memory of them eventually faded away into the veiled cobwebs of myth and legend as the new age emerged.

During her years alone, Sarah was supported by a wide circle of friends throughout the community. But it was her friendship with the Blanchards in Mobile that kept her life centered on an even keel. She made the trip to Mobile as often as her failing health allowed and saw Hanna grow up under the kind care of Ken and Abigail.

Abigail had been faithful to their friendship. She knew how much John and Sarah had loved Hanna. She wrote Sarah often after John had died. She would tell her what wonderful things Hanna was doing and the extraordinary woman she was becoming.

She told her that John, as a physician, would have been so proud of the work Hanna was doing in Mobile's hospitals accompanying her as a nurse. She remembered that Hanna had accompanied John on his rounds when she was so little.

She told her that they wished they could make the trip more often to see her. She offered hope that Hanna, as a grown woman, would come up on her own.

Nine - Mobile

The Blanchards had settled their lives in Mobile long before the Civil War. Ken was a business man with a thriving import and export business even before the war had begun. They took Hanna Drish into their care near the end of the war.

Mobile had been part of Mississippi but joined prominently Protestant Alabama and became a diocese of the Roman Catholic Church, likely due to its French and Spanish origins and orientation as an upriver port to the Gulf of Mexico, and second only to New Orleans. In 1847, the Jesuit Order took over the Spring Hill College established earlier in 1830.

Early in the Civil War, Admiral Farragut had blockaded Mobile's port, which had been heavily fortified by the Confederates, and cut off commerce from the outside. Food, raw materials, cloth and other sundries were in short supply. Women gathered on Spring Hill Road and stormed up Dauphin Street with brooms and axes and banners demanding bread or blood.

In August of '64 his warships fought their way past Fort Gaines and Fort Morgan and defeated Confederate gunboats. Mobile was not defeated but was isolated. The end came in April of '65 when the city of Mobile was overrun by Federal forces, couldn't hold out any longer, and surrendered.

During the last quarter of the 19th century, Mobile was in turmoil. The Reconstructionist Republicans held control of her in 1867. In 1874, Democrats used violence and extreme measures to wrest control of the city back and keep African Americans and non-

Democrats from voting. By 1875, the Democrats had put the city into decline.

Ken Blanchard was a Catholic and a slave owner, but operated under a different situation than those on the cotton plantations. He and Abigail lived in a large mansion in the city with household slaves who were charged with all the household operations and had a degree of autonomy. The slaves outside the homestead worked as dock hands, stevedores and warehouse workers for the Blanchard Import-Export Company.

While appearing similar to the living patterns on the rural plantations, the two groups were adapted to a closer, more intimate urban setting. Their surroundings in the city – those inside and those outside the household - were more crowded and there was less land to spread out spacious areas for slave cabins. Well before emancipation, living together closer as they did, there was more democracy, as well as intimacy between the slaves and their white owners.

Ken had discussed these subtle differences in relationships with John Drish on several occasions.

When John and Sarah came to visit, he often said, "We have to live with them closer than you do, so we necessarily form closer relationships. It seems to work out for the best."

Eventually though, as Mobile developed, there was a section provided by the group of business owners that was entirely allocated for housing the slaves. As they became more like dayworkers, the intimacy diminished. They had their own neighborhood for their own kind.

The women of the black families still worked as domestics in the owner's households, while the men worked away and outside on the docks and in the warehouses. A few black families still lived right behind the city mansion lots and were more closely available to the white owners as virtually live-in servants.

When the slaves were freed, the sections of town that were entirely inhabited by them became the black side of town. In reality, the only difference for them was that they were paid to work and required to pay for their housing. They became the city version of the small tenant farmers established after the end of the war.

The Blanchards had slaves in their household and maintained a small compound of cabins at the back of their property for the slaves that worked for them as stevedores and warehouse workers at the waterfront docks.

Eventually Ken joined too with the other businessmen to pool their resources and help build the neighborhood of brick buildings for the aggregated slave family housing. After the war and emancipation, African Americans went out to work for wages and had their own place where they were on their own. They belonged to themselves.

When John and Sarah Drish arrived at the Blanchards' with Hanna, Ken and Abigail were surprised to see a shy, nicely dressed Negro child, hiding behind Sarah's skirts. Their telegram had been cryptic but implied a serious matter. As old friends, they trusted each other implicitly so they welcomed the threesome into their home.

The Blanchards couldn't help but notice how quiet and sad Hanna was. She did not seem like most 8 year old children they had met or known. Abigail suggested that perhaps Hanna could go into the kitchen with the cook and have something to eat while they talked in the parlor.

John and Sarah told Ken and Abigail about the slave revolt and Josena's unfortunate death. John was visibly upset that his slaves whom he had always treated kindly could do something like that – more so when their beloved Josena had been senselessly killed.

"I couldn't have imagined that would happen, Ken. We loved Josena and were devastated when she was needlessly killed in an instant. She was a member of our family. And now poor Hanna who never knew her father, has lost her mother. She was born to us and has spent her whole life with us.

But then, in a matter of days, our tattered Confederate defenders were rushing to the outside of town to meet the Yankees. Their artillery pressed closer and their forces overwhelmed us so fast, so furiously and so deadly. We didn't know how they would treat us, or our property, so we had to hasten and escape to safety."

Ken was saddened by John's words, thought for a moment and said, "I can see how close you have become to Hanna and why. I have always known you to care for people and care about them."

"She has come with me to visit and tend to my patients. She's very special, Ken. There's something odd about her too. There is a spiritual aura about her I can't understand. It's almost eerie. She seems to know things a little child couldn't possibly know or understand. I just know she has captured my heart."

"What are you going to do?" Ken asked.

"Sometimes when you love someone so much, you have to let them go. It's for the best. I don't feel she would be safe with us now after all that has happened. I want you and Abigail to take her and raise her. I trust you completely. She needs your protection and your safety."

Abigail offered, "The Union forces have occupied our port and city for over a year now. They control everything and Ken has had to work with them to keep our business going. They are our customer now. But it is peaceful here and we have no fear of being burned out or killed."

Ken asked her, "What do you think Abby? I'd like to take Hanna if you would undertake it."

She saw the tears running down Sarah's face, looked back at Ken and said, "Of course I would. She will be one of our own."

John held Sarah's hand, looked at her and smiled. The Blanchards could almost hear their sigh of relief.

Ken said, "Don't worry dear friends. This will be her safe harbor."

Sarah said, "We are relieved and in your debt. Now we need to prepare Hanna for this big change in her life. She just lost her mother a few days ago and she is very distraught. That's why she appears so quiet and shy here today.

She is very smart and loves her bible. You will come to love the real Hanna once she becomes adjusted."

Now it was time to talk to Hanna. She was so mature in many ways, it was sometimes hard to remember that she was just a little girl. These last days she had been so quiet it was hard to know what she was thinking or how she was doing with her loss.

Abigail went into the kitchen and brought her into the parlor. Hanna sensed that the adults seemed very serious and that frightened her. She clung tightly onto Abigail's hand, not sure what was about to happen.

She vaguely remembered seeing the Blanchards years ago when they visited the Drish plantation, but they were still strangers to her. Her heart was beating rapidly and she was fighting to keep back the tears that threatened to flow.

She missed her mama. As she remembered her though, a sudden calm entered her consciousness. It was as if she could feel her mother's arms around her telling her that everything would be alright and that she would always be there in her heart for as long as she lived.

Hanna entered the parlor and went to sit by John Drish, looking with wide eyes at everyone in the room.

John took her hand and gently said, "Look at me child. You know that Sarah and I love you just as we loved your mother. We are so sorry that we couldn't keep her safe, but now we want to make sure that you are safe and have a good home.

You remember the Blanchards, they came and visited us a few years ago. They have this beautiful home in the city and two children who are just a little older than you. They would like you to come and live here with them here in this house and help out just as you did at our house. We promise to come visit you from time to time. We just want you to be happy and safe. What do you think?"

No one had ever asked Hanna what she wanted to do. She didn't know what to think or say. But somewhere inside her a little voice was telling her to do what the Drishs wanted. So she just shyly nodded her head yes and waited for one of the grownups to say something more.

Abigail Blanchard came over, sat beside her, took her hand and said, "Hanna, we really want you to come and live with us. We know you will be happy here. So welcome home child."

The Drishs needed to get back to the plantation. They had left hurriedly and with the situation the way it was, they didn't want to be gone long. So they gave Hanna a big hug and left to go home. Hanna watched from the porch as their carriage went down the street. She felt so alone, but like her mother, she squared her shoulders and went to face her new life with a smile on her face.

Just two years later, when Hanna was ten years old, John Drish died suddenly in a tragic accident. Grief-stricken, Sarah sent word by telegram to Ken and Abigail. They hurriedly packed up some things and, with Hanna accompanying them, drove their carriage to Tuscaloosa to be at Sarah's side and comfort her.

As they approached the Drish house, Hanna remembered it from just two years ago when she had left. From her earliest recollections, she remembered the extensive addition John's slave William had put on it just before the war had come to Tuscaloosa. The columns in the front were magnificent and the place looked like a great castle to her young eyes. The iron work on the new porches was unique. There was nothing like it she had ever seen. It was certainly different from the city mansions where she lived now.

They found Sarah so lost to reality that they took over John's final arrangements. They asked what her wishes were for memorializing him.

"Contact Prince Murrell", was all she could say.

Reverend Murrell was the pastor of the new First African Baptist Church on Stillman Boulevard and a friend of the Drish's for most of their lives. The new church had humble origins moving from Hood's Mill and Barr's store to its own permanent building on Stillman. There would be a long history of Christian scholarship to follow Murrell's footsteps with a succession of prominent pastors, including one graduate of Tuskegee Institute and another of McGill University in Canada.

The friendships reached across racial barriers all the way back to when the Murrels had first attended the old First Baptist Church with blacks and whites attending in equal numbers – all of Tuscaloosa's Christian people.

Sarah knew that Reverend Murrell was a kind man who would give solace to the community of Tuscaloosa. Everyone held him in high esteem. Hannah had fresh memories of the Reverend teaching Sunday school to her and the other children.

The community came out in full numbers for the service to give John a reverent sendoff. The Reverend gave the eulogy and many got up to share his memory. Sarah was pleased and, through her tears, felt their love.

Before they left for home, the Blanchards visited Sarah one last time to say their goodbyes. Remembering the sad past history, they led Hanna out to the yard behind the Drish house and the small gated cemetery there. She knelt down at her mother's gravesite looking at the headstone. They read the words on the stone, "Josena- Beloved House Girl – Died September 1864".

The Blanchards stood there in a moment of reverent silence while Hanna knelt at the gravesite and prayed, "Oh Mama, I miss ya so. Give ha peace at last Lord. She was a good Cristchen wuman. Doan worry 'bout me. I'se doin' fine Mama. People tekin' care of me good. I love you Mama."

Ken rested his hand lightly on her shoulder and smiled lovingly into her face. He and Abigail, one on each hand, led Hanna away.

Sarah Drish was alone and lonely in the big house on 17th Street after John was gone. Her grief consumed her and her sadness never subsided. The neighbors and the community did what they could – what she would accept and tolerate. She kept her spirits up the best she could.

She told her servant to harness up the carriage and she set out for Mobile to see the Blanchards. He drove her there in the good weather and felt better he could do something for her. They stayed in the mansion on Dauphin Street – he in the servants' quarters.

Ken and Abigail enjoyed her visits and reminisced about the old days when they were young and coming up.

"That was just a moment ago", Sarah said.

Hanna was so happy to see Sarah again and they renewed their care and concern for each other. Sarah was old now but Hanna remembered the days with her in Tuscaloosa and the love they shared.

"Wonderful to see ya mama Sarah", she said. "I missed you and the good days in your house. Its bin so long."

"How grown up you have become", she said.

It warmed Sarah's heart to see Hanna growing up and becoming the young woman she was. But she remembered. She thought how it was when she was so little - her tragic loss and how brave she was.

Hanna thought about Sarah often after John died. She talked about it with Abigail.

"Maybe I shud go up thereah and be wid ha'", she said.

Abigail told her, "There is a limit to how much you can do – for her and yourself. She comes down here when she can and seems fine for a grieving widow. She's doing all right and you have much to do here."

"Maybe you right Abigail. Wid your daughters grown 'n' gone, maybe I stay hereah wid you."

"We want you here and we have work to do together at the hospitals", Abigail reassured her.

Abigail didn't have a sense about Sarah's failing health. Hanna stayed.

During their troubled times, like everyone else, the Blanchards made do. They participated in trade with the blockade runners when they could or traded with the Federals when there was that opportunity. It was tenuous either way.

Abigail believed in the southern cause and way of life. She was active in charity for the many new poor and wounded spawned from the "War of Northern Aggression". As an affluent and patriotic citizen, she helped out where she could. She rolled bandages and cared for the wounded. She went weekly to the sewing circle of her church and helped make clothing and blankets to be given to those in need.

She volunteered at Mobile City Hospital to care for civilians with yellow fever, cholera and other diseases. She volunteered at the Marine Hospital for Confederate soldiers who were wounded or ill. She learned something about herself – that she got fulfillment from caring for others in need. She enjoyed nursing.

With her two daughters cared for in her home or away at school, she spent whole days at the hospitals – arriving after breakfast and staying until just before dinner. She believed she was helping the war effort and it was a great satisfaction.

She learned about the medicines administered in her day. Since aspirin would not be synthesized until 1897, there was just willow bark tea for the treatment of headache and mild pain. Paracetamol became available in 1887 for treatment of mild pain also. Laudanum – opium dissolved in alcohol – was used since 1800 for cough and pain.

For severe pain, morphine, made from poppy plants, had been in wide use since 1827 and through the Civil War. Many young soldiers had become addicted from its overuse. General Grant wrote his memoirs while using Vin Mariani, a cocaine infused wine, to keep awake and for pain from his throat cancer.

Morphine became available, as a form of opium disguised in various tonics, from the Sears catalog. Doctors and nurses however, administered it by hypodermic syringe when that was invented in 1853.

For the Yellow Fever, not much could be done except for treatment of its symptoms. Without saline IV, rehydration was accomplished by administering drinking water. Without anti-viral drugs, aspirin was administered when it became available.

Abigail learned about these medicines and treatments as she became a recognized nurse. While practicing her skills, she was sensitive to the trauma Hanna must have endured from her mother's death and uprooting from the Drish house to the Blanchards here in Mobile.

She often brought little Hanna with her. It became apparent very quickly that for Hanna it was a calling, more than a satisfactory cause. John Drish sensed this from the earliest when he brought her with him on his doctor visits. Hanna had a gentle light and a sensitive touch that soothed the suffering of the patients. It was a reassurance to them when she touched their face or their hands. A peace and a calm came over them when they looked at her face.

Long after the war, as Hanna grew older, she learned the practicalities of nursing from Abigail, just as Abigail had learned them before. Together they continued to heal the sick and infirm.

For her religious upbringing, Hanna had learned the rituals and formality of Christianity in the Catholic Church with the Blanchards. When she became a teenager and had accepted her covenant with God, she began attending the African Methodist Episcopal Church with other African Americans. The AME worship was more personal, more emotional, and more soulful. It fit better with her nature. There she learned God's love and His purpose. She better understood her purpose and how to fulfill her promise.

As she grew to adulthood, Hanna had read her bible in its entirety so many times that she had nearly committed its words to memory. She was often called upon to give brief sermons at the AME Church. The African American community knew her as a spiritually gifted woman of God and often called upon her to visit when a member was ailing in body or spirit.

With their growing concerns for social justice and racial equality, the African Americans in Mobile often sought violence in retaliation for violence in their frustration for equal treatment. Hanna told them that the path to freedom was faith. She suggested to the angry leaders that the churches should became the epicenters for the leadership fighting for civil rights. To be successful, it would be done peacefully and with passive resistance.

She reassured them of her certainty that God would guide them with His providence to find the goodness in people of both races. It could be done only that way – with the hearts of good people coming together. God had shown her this truth. She continued to follow her mission well into her twenties.

Eventually, with the early experience she had gained as a child with John Drish and the mature experience and practice at the Mobile hospitals, Hanna was paid a stipend for her healing work. She was able to save some money of her own. It was purely a practical matter. Hanna had never paid much attention to or cared about money.

Mobile

Ten – God's Reflection

I thought about the order of things as I have made them,

'The angels are My most sentient beings. They watch the humans and are aware of their actions and thoughts. But they do not act without My direction. The thousand thousand of them are but a few compared to the numbers of the humans.

They follow the commands of their leaders, the archangels, I have placed before them. I have given my archangels some freedom to act on their own just as I have given the humans. But unlike the humans, my archangels understand My wishes completely. I can trust in their spirits.

Only once did I cast one of them out of the heavens. He rebuked My authority and so I banished him to the netherworld. He resides in the dark places of the earth and in the hearts of some of the humans.

I have permitted him to continue to exist and serve as the source of evil in the world. Rather than destroy him, I have kept him to suit Me. He is needed in the balance of things.

He has tempted the lowly humans as a test for their devotion to Me. When they do rebuke him, they prove their worthiness to Me. For I have created them with free will knowing that they would struggle with the evil within them and strive to find the goodness.

And so it will always be that the humans will carry good and evil in their hearts. Each will become what they choose to become. Only those that overcome their evil, and are good, will I reward.'

When I spoke to Michael, he told Me about the birth of the slave girl, Hanna born on Earth. He had come to Me out of fear for her – how she would spend the span of terrestrial life given to her.

He said to me, "Yahweh, this little one must be salvaged. I see in her spirit the promise of goodness. I wish to visit her when she is older and command her to bring her spirit to the humans in her war-torn country. I seek your permission to use her for our purposes."

I thought for a moment,
'Michael - he of the terrible swift sword - most often seeks violent methods to solve problems with the humans. His nature since I created him has been to do battle against evil. He rarely has interest in the cultivation of goodness. Usually he is impatient and chooses to fight. He has always done so over the eons.

Gabriel has the lighter touch. Even Raphael and Uriel take the gentler approach to My missions. Usually I use Michael in times of a great war when My might is most needed. But Michael has come to Me. He has found this little one. Perhaps it will be different this time. Perhaps it will be good for Michael to act for peace – for him to learn patience and avoid the temptation to fight. This Hanna must be special to have attracted his interest.

Michael has always been my greatest warrior in our continuing war that the humans know nothing of – the war between good and evil. The battleground has been the Earth with the humans as the unwitting participants. The forces from the heavens have met those of the underworld there and Michael has led My angels into the struggles unseen by My humans. But now he is inspired by this insignificant human child.'

I have made my decision Michael. When she reaches the age of budding womanhood, before she becomes bound to a man for the remainder of her life, go to her. Use the wisdom I have bestowed on you and give her the mission to act for our goodness and mercy. Bind her with her vow to spend her lifespan working for my plan. Go when it is time and watch her life closely. I want you to tell Me where she prevails and where she fails.

I thought once again,

'I saw right from the beginning when Eve bore her sons Cain and Abel that the humans were given to jealousy and anger. Cain was the first to be born of human and Abel the first to die under human hands.

I made my covenant with Abraham and he founded the great nation of Israel. Then he sired his sons, Ismael and later Isaac when he was one hundred of the years they use to measure time. They founded the two great religions from their tribes. But they fought over their differences in faith and so acted falsely to Me.

I remember the conflict between the brothers Jacob and Esau over the birthright from their father Isaac. Born together from their mother Rebekah, all their descendent nations were at war and separated over the selfishness, deception and greed of her sons. They made war and wasted human life.

But these are my greatest species that dwell on the Earth. I require they care for each other, shepherd the animals and tend to the land. I knew that my creatures would try to bring themselves to ruin - that there would always be tribal strife. For many days of their time they would try to bring cataclysm upon themselves.

I often intervened in small ways caring for them so much as I do. But I leave their destiny on My Earth in their hands. That was what I decided.

I have seen many men who are unaware that they are filled with the spirit of evil. Very few have professed it openly and consciously.

Many others have invoked My name and have believed their actions brought glory to it. Some might be forgiven for their transgressions for their hearts were pure. Robert E. Lee, Thomas Jackson, Ulysses Grant and William Sherman were such men – good men, honorable men, moral, pious, with righteousness and rectitude, dutiful to their cause as they believed their cause to be, loyal to their men, consistent in their belief in Me until their deaths. When they had done all they could do to prepare for their great battles, they professed that then it was in My hands.

But they have broken My 6th commandment – they have killed, committed murder. This is a grievous sin no matter what their cause had been. In other times it was I who commanded tribes of peoples to rise up and smite their enemies without mercy. My chosen people of the twelve tribes of Israel were told to do this when they were forming their great nation. This case with the Americans is like that.

It depends on My judgment and I am Yahweh, the One true God.

As long as they know that it is wrong to kill My children and ask for forgiveness, I can forgive them.

I created all and only I can judge all and forgive.

I must forgive them.

I see that Hanna must be girded for confrontation, for she will face the evil of men like Nathan Bedford Forrest. She must deter them with her spirit as her only weapon. I know that when that happens I will be at her side and she will prevail. It is the meek that I love the most and they must survive.'

Michael said to me, "It shall be done Lord. I will watch over her and protect her. She will be one of us and use your power of Love to wage her battles."

I saw that it was done.

I watched with disinterest as the hurricane began to form up in the Caribbean. I spun it up and pushed it west and then northwest as it passed Florida. It struck land across the Gulf at Baton Rouge. I was angry at the South and felt like punishing it for its transgressions. But I thought better of myself and wound it down after it made landfall.

I just gave them a week of black sky and miserable rain. It suited My mood. They were too pitiful to bring down My wrath. Let Michael and the others see what they can do.

I'm not angry really. I don't feel any fire or passion. I'm just in a bad mood – kind of disappointed, despondent and feeling some despair. It's fatigue. I'm just tired. It's happening more and more now that I am getting so old.

I don't require blood sacrifice anymore. That was mostly their idea to prove their worthiness anyway. All I have ever required is that they love me and each other.

Micah told them all that I require when he said, "He hath shewed thee, O man, what is good; and what doth the Lord require of thee, but to do justly, and to love mercy, and walk humbly with thy God."

It's been a tiresome day for Me – this history of America. It started out with such promise when I sent the people across the land bridge to populate the new continent.

When the Europeans first came, they brought such cruelty to My children. They claimed to do it in My name. Then the others came with so much moral piety and devotion to Me. Their intentions and plans were filled with such goodness. But then they turned to cruelty again. I can't help but think it was better for them before they tasted the tree of knowledge. It was simpler. Now the moments of peace are so short lived.

I have relied on My messengers to advise the humans to choose the true path. But, as I reflect on the humans and what that has done, I think about their past and the old ways then. I looked into their souls, into the darkest places of despondence and hopelessness. There I struck with light – so bright I blinded them with the truth. There was nothing visible to them but a universe of pure white light. It was the goodness they were needing. I reached them that way then, all of them, even the darkest, even the ones farthest away, and they knew.

I will rest. Tomorrow will be a better day.

The rain has stopped. There, there is a rainbow.

Eleven - Michael

Red clay dust from the road covered her legs and the hem of her white dress. Perspiration ran down her face and its salt burned her eyes. The cotton fields were empty. She had been walking for days and hadn't seen a living soul by the time she crossed the border from Alabama into Mississippi yesterday.

"Oh Lord, I is so thirsty", she muttered as her field of vision grew narrower and darker in the bright afternoon sun.

Hanna stumbled off the road and lay down on the edge of the field. Her heartbeat slowed down as she fell into a deep sleep.

The recurring dream came back again as it had for more than a year. The big man in the white linen caftan looked sternly, seriously and with resolve, but his eyes were loving as he stood over her once again.

"I'm your father, girl. We have never met but I have been with you always."

His deeply lined face looked like hers as he smiled, backed away and waved goodbye.

She had felt compelled to travel west in the direction of the sunset. There was something there she would find. It would be important, she felt.

Her eyes opened and the farmer was standing there over her with concern on his face. He wore a wide brimmed felt hat and dusty coveralls over his rolled up cotton shirt. The straps and the bib from his coveralls hung down his legs and in front of his waist and his shirt was opened wide down the front of his chest. He took off his hat and his curly dark hair glistened with sweat on his head and his chest.

"Are you alright wuman?" he asked.

"I couldn't tell if you was alive 'cept for yo' faint breathin."

Hanna said, "Kin I get a drink a watah?"

He smiled with relief and said, "Let me hep you up and tek you to my house. It's coolah."

A day earlier out of Mobile she had heard a feint thunder of hoofs ahead up the road. As a cloud of dust arose, she saw a group of men riding toward her. There were about five of them wearing old gray Confederate tunics. They had a rough look about them. She thought right away they were a group of KKK raiders on the prowl and she was in danger.

In a moment they had surrounded her carriage and forced her to pull up on the reins and stop.

She was quiet and calm and showed no fear.

With distain on his curled lips, one of the men said, "Well looky here at this fine nigger woman. Where are you goin' in yo pretty dress?"

She calmly held him in a steady gaze.

"You look like you ready fo' a fight", he continued.

She finally answered, “Goin’ west.”

The man asked again, “Where to?

Hanna just said, “Mississippi, I ‘spose.”

Another man, young with a red beard, agreed she looked feisty, “Let’s have us sum fun. I ain’t had no juicy dark meat in a while. I luvta watch the disagreeable ones squirm.”

She ignored him and looked at the older one with the long dark beard and the cold black eyes. He hadn’t said anything but she could tell he was the one in charge.

He saw something in her steady stare that made him pause and have doubt.

“No, leave her be. We have somewherah to go and don’t have the time.”

Red beard said, “Nathan, it won’t tek us long. We been ridin’ hard. We needs some receashun.”

His horse became agitated and whinnied. It pawed the ground with its front hooves, bounced up and down on them and reared up on its hind legs. Red beard struggled with the reins until his horse stood still once again.

Forrest watched curiously, with disinterest, almost indifferently, and repeated again, “I said leave her be. Take her horse and wagon and leave her heah.”

N.B. Forrest had never backed down in war. In fact he charged forward in battle, often ahead of his cavalry, at full gallop, slashing his sword at the enemy, without regard for his own safety, and with all odds stacked heavily against him. He never backed down. He was either one of the bravest or the most deluded the South had ever produced.

He had believed that Grant and Sherman were wrong – that he was on the side of right – the side of the Constitution. So the superior numbers didn't dissuade him, nor the superior armaments either. And neither fatigue nor hunger dissuaded his men from following him.

The Union underestimated the depth of this belief as they faced opponents like Forrest, James Longstreet, Pierre Beauregard and Albert Johnston and Tom Jackson before they were killed. The Confederates were fighting for something, not against something. They were imbued with old romantic notions of chivalry and glory which, as nonsensical as they were, empowered them to victory in many battles they rightfully should not have won.

But that was during the war. And that had all come to ruin. It wasn't for God and country anymore.

Now he was leading a small ragtag band of malcontents and losers. There was no winning the lost cause. He had changed from the flamboyant cavalry soldier to this embittered and hateful man.

In this encounter today, with this pitiful ex-slave woman, there was no honor – no victory to gain – nothing to win. Red beard's horse had acted curiously. That didn't make any sense.

"Let her go", he had said. He rode away ahead of his men with indifference – alone in his thoughts.

They grabbed her arm, flung her to the ground and dumped her carpetbag beside her on the road. They went off on their way with one of them driving her carriage and another holding the reins of his rider-less horse.

Hanna, got up and watched them ride out of sight. Her shoulder and backside were sore but she knew she still had her bible in her bag. “Thank you Lord”, she said.

She sat down on the side of the road and watched down its distance as the riders disappeared and the dust dissipated. She was alone and in silence except for the steady buzz of the cicadas in the fields. The sky far off toward the horizon just above the roadbed shimmered as the midday heat rose from the surface.

She stared at them as they vanished and thought, ‘I had believed in showing mercy to others. God had taught me to do that. But when it was my turn to be shown mercy, I surrendered all belief in mercy. Then mercy was granted to me.’

In her thoughts she wondered, ‘He has seen so much of human livin’, now that He is old. He has watched and witnessed so much lustful sinnin’, greed, cruelty and despair. So much unnecessary killin’ and death. So much immorality, selfishness, arrogance and indifference. Only God could love us after all that. Only God could still smile upon us and make a rainbow, now that He is old.’

She got up after a long while and continued down the road on foot. The blazing sun and oppressive heat sapped her energy as she walked along tugging her carpet bag beside her in the dust. She came to a greener area, collapsed under a shade tree and immediately fell into a deep sleep. In a dream Michael came to her once again.

Michael

He stood towering over her and smiled without uttering a word. There was just his brilliant white visage looking down upon her, comforting her.

She cried out to him in a language of thought clearer than she could ever speak out loud, “Why does the Lord allow humans to act so cruelly to one another? Why has He given us that free will?”

He squatted down and balanced on his heels so that he could be closer to her as she lay on the ground. He smiled at her conveying his love.

“Why doesn’t He just make us obey His will?” she asked.

After a long silence Michael spoke, “God made that choice long ago when you tasted of the tree of knowledge. He gave you free will because you have a soul Hanna. Your soul is His gift and it means human beings have free will.”

“But some humans use their free will in defiance of the Word”, she thought.

She felt his love and had no fear of him. She just wanted to understand.

Michael understood her need and spoke again, “The Word is God. He has given it to you. Hanna, your faith is a choice. And if faith is a choice, it can be lost – for a man, an angel or the devil himself.”

He waited while she thought.

“You have been faithful and God is pleased with the direction you have taken to keep your covenant with Him. There is more for you to understand. God has sent me to you again because it is time for you to learn more.”

“Tell me angel. I want to know what I must do.”

Michael was pleased she was ready and said, “My kind understand His purpose more completely and follow the Word without free will. Faith is not needed for us. He has made us this way.”

“We are given certain powers not of the Earth, but not free will. You see that we have no need for it. We have knowledge of Him and so do not need faith either.”

"Your kind will never understand God's plan completely. But understanding part of it as you do, your part, is what it means to have a soul. In the end that is what being a human being is about. With your soul you can love. That is His gift to you" he continued.

"When your life of this Earth is completed – when He decides it is time - you will share our immortality."

Hanna smiled full into his face.

"But while you live in this mortal coil, He has commanded me to give you a power only a few humans possess."

He reached out his hand and said, "Take my hand".

She was not fearful exactly, more like timid and awestruck, as she tentatively took his hand.

When she did, he asked, "Do you feel that?"

She felt a slight electrical tingle and nodded to him in affirmation.

"You are given the power to heal with your touch. God has said that this will strengthen your mission with those you will encounter. In many cases, your touch will heal their illness. In every case, they will feel His love through your instrument."

Michael reached into his robe and held out an orange in his hand.

"I was helping the humans in Florida after the hurricane and picked this up for you. Take this and eat it", he said. "I have no use for food and you are in need of nourishment."

She held it in her hand and it was cool. She peeled and ate it. It soothed her dry throat.

"One thing before I go. I heard that you were concerned that God is old, maybe he is too tired to care anymore. I have it on good authority that is not true. He is timeless and ageless. Time as you know it has no meaning for Him. The world had a beginning and will have an end. But He had no beginning and will have no end."

At last Saint Michael told her what she needed to know and said,

"Hanna, the time has come to tell you the pure truth and its essence – God's truth. It is more than your God-given mission and the covenant you made with Him when you were a young girl – for harmony among people. It is beyond that and more deeply rooted in understanding what is man and what is God.

You are old enough, strong enough and wise enough now to know it. So here is the truth of it, all of it.

God has forever watched man, His creation. He has seen all things. He knows man's frailties in every way and beyond what you can imagine – man is mendacious, selfish, thieving, murderous, warmongering, power-seeking, lustful, fornicating, sinful, immoral, narcissistic, self-centered, self-motivated, arrogant, cruel, tribal, petty, unilluminated, untranscendent, unfeeling, uncaring, heartless, mindless, ignorant and blind - and knows the essence of the meaning of human life.

How could God let man be these things? It is because He has given him free will and man is not God. He has expected him to listen. He has expected him to understand. Many have done this. Many have not.

I give you this now on His authority. You know what it is. When I tell you, you will already know that you know it. It is love."

Michael stood and began to move away. His brilliance rose and blended into the light from the sun until he was no longer visible. She awakened under the cool shade of the tree.

Hanna had known that to love is good and that it pleased the Lord. But now she knew three more things. She knew that God wanted us to love each other for certain, and that God is love and when that is known for certain, that is grace – God's grace. Now she was illuminated, risen up, transcended, and forever imbued with His Spirit.

Twelve - McComb

All across Mississippi she saw the devastation of the land and the gaunt lost look in the eyes of its people – the scattered few she encountered. Both black and white, they were starving and had no hope.

As Hanna began her traverse of Mississippi, about a week or two out of Mobile, she met a couple heading in the other direction. They were an elderly white couple in a fine carriage and dressed more refined than anyone she had seen in the region.

She hailed them with a smile and upraised hand and said, "'Scuse me folks. I sees ya goin' east. Wheah ya headed?"

They told her they were going to Alabama – to Mobile.

"Tha's a blessin", she told them. "Would ya does me a favah ifs ya cans?"

They were decent people and were willing to help.

"Please wudya look up de Blanchards on Dauphin Street whens ya theah? Tell 'em they Hanna fine 'n' doin' well comin' 'cros Mississippi."

They smiled and promised they would. So Ken and Abigail, still mystified about Hanna's departure, knew she was well.

When she eventually arrived in McComb, Mississippi, she found a small quiet town without much activity. The local people didn't move around very much, or very quickly. There was little to do and the steamy humidity of the nearby swamp forested area discouraged strenuous effort. There was no relief and no breezes coming in from cooler bodies of water either.

For Hanna, this was much different than Mobile for certain, but harkened back to her childhood long ago in Tuscaloosa. The people were friendly enough to a stranger. Their curiosity about her broke the tedium.

She talked to a man at the general store. In country towns, this was the place to get information and even the place to send and receive mail. The man was at the small counter serving as the local post office when she approached him.

"Good aftanoon", she said. "Knows any place Ah cud stays whiles Ah's heah?"

He told her there was one boardinghouse but not for coloreds like her.

"Theys a colored famly wud put ya up 'n' feed ya ifs ya wants."

"Thank ya kindly mista", she said.

He gave her their name and she went on her way.

Hanna met a local, a white man, on the street and declared, "Ah come heah ta look fo' work."

The white man she met was of middle age and was clean of appearance. She didn't mention she had some money saved up with her.

"Does ya knows any folks who needs someun ta care fo' they youngins, or keep they house, or needs sum healin' fo' they ailmens?"

She didn't want to tell a stranger a greater mission had driven her to this place, or at least in this direction, or how it had come to be.

He suggested, "Theys sum folks cud use that. Reckon Ah cain't think 'bout any names jus now."

"Thank ya sah. You kind to a strangah. De otha thang is Ah thinks my mama she come from heah long 'go, back bafor' tha war. Ah thinks shes on a plantation round heah."

He looked at this pleasant black woman, nearing middle age herself, and remembered, "Yas. Theys a plantation heah onct. Called it Savannah Oaks."

"Oh my stars, how does Ah find it?"

He pointed in two directions.

"Ya see dat road ova theah? Dat's tha ole road bafor' they be puttin' tha new un ova heah."

She looked at the overgrown narrow path leading away from town.

"It go jus 'bout haf mile ta tha ole place. Ya can 'most see hit from heah. Not much ta see theah tho'. Jus a ole broke down buildin' 'n' some wreak cabins. Use' ta be, 'afor tha town built, right heah was part ov tha plantation."

She thanked him kindly and trudged double time out the old road. The man watched her go, amazed at her speed in this damnable heat. When she came up to the mansion, she saw it wasn't as bad as the man had described it. It was shaded dark with the huge live oaks.

The house was still beautiful and majestic, but overgrown so much with vines and green vegetation. Nature has taken its toll in just a few decades, but not completely.

The slave cabins were mostly rotten and fallen apart from the incessant onslaught of the humidity and moisture.

She stopped there and soberly reflected, 'This must be where my father lived with my mother so long ago.'

She became saddened and she cried. She prayed for their immortal souls.

Hanna stayed in McComb. It felt right to be close to the memory of Savannah Oaks. Before long, she began to meet the people there and began to find ways to help them. She began to settle In. The people of both races liked her; became drawn to her.

She did begin to keep their houses, and look after their children, and take care of their sick, and give spiritual solace to their dying. They came to see her gentle light and she made them happier and more at peace with their lives.

Before very long, she turned to the African Methodist Episcopal church there for her solace and spiritual sustenance. It gave her a community of sympathetic souls.

Hanna met an old woman named Nora Travers who lived on the edge of town just south off the main road. Some folks in town thought the wrinkled, stooped over old white woman was a witch. It was because Nora spent her time foraging for roots and herbs and brewing healing potions.

When Hanna found her, they struck up a friendship. Hanna knew there was much she could learn from her new friend. Nora could see the kind goodness in Hanna and that Hanna accepted her for what she was.

They became dearest friends with the common mission of healing. Nora had a bountiful knowledge of how to cure the body's ailments. Hanna had a gift for healing the tortured and hateful soul.

They foraged together in the fields and the forest and tended the herbal garden around Nora's old ramshackle cabin.

"Now lookit dis deah", Nora told her in her creaky, almost inaudible voice.

"Hit's call fevahfew 'n' hits good fo' headaches, fevah, so' bones, sick stumick 'n' wumen's time ov month."

Hanna remembered and told her, "Ah knows 'bout willow bark 'n' how hits hepful fo' tha aches 'n' tha fevah too.

"Ah gets dat from tha willa trees in da swamp. Ah shaves tha bark 'n' boils hit up ina tea", she said.

"Us learns 'bout dis from da animals", she continued.

Hanna asked her what she was growing in the garden.

Nora said, "Ah gots mint 'n' chamomile good fo' tha digestin. Sumtime mix wid tha sage 'n' tha thyme ta mek hit taste bettah. Gots ta be careful 'bout sum thins like poison hemlock n' nightshade. Cud kill ya if'n ya donts know wat ya doin'."

Nora gave her a small leather satchel with a string she had made so that Hanna could keep her herbs and roots around her neck when she visited the people. Hanna wore it next to her necklace with the cross. Both of these vestiges meant healing to Hanna.

They spent so much time there together at Nora's place that she invited Hanna to come live with her. Hanna was happy to have a place to live and a friend for companionship. The two of them became inseparable there.

But Nora, as a recluse, preferred to stay at her home tending her garden, while Hanna spent most of her time with the people in McComb – looking after them and taking care of them. The little money she took more than provided for her and Nora's modest needs. They lived simply and purely.

Hanna never missed Sunday worship unless she was tending the sick. The Lord would understand that. It fulfilled her, and was her joy, to hear the word, to read from the book, to sing and to pray, and to laugh and to cry.

When she ministered to the sick and applied her herbal remedies, Hanna laid her hands on her patients and said a prayer. They came to recognize that she had a spirit – a special way about her – that was not to be feared but to be cherished. It was goodness and based on love.

Hanna was not above doing the hard work of cleaning the folks' houses, or doing their laundry, or the smart work of caring for their children. She got to know everybody that way.

Word spread about her among people of the region and she was sought after. Many wanted to just be with her, in her presence. God was grateful for Michael's initiative and He was smiling.

By 1888, she had been living and working in McComb for many years. She had heard about the crazy old woman who lived by herself and spooked the town folk. She went to visit her and took pity on her.

She smiled calmly at her while the old woman kept talking about thievin' niggers right to her face - as though she was not even there or that she didn't even look just like the people the woman was babbling about. It was a test of her faith. She acted mercifully as she had been taught, as she practiced, as she believed.

Hanna had no way of knowing that this was the woman who had been so cruel to her mother Josena when she had been a child under the woman's control. The old woman had no way of knowing that this kind woman was the daughter of the same Josena she had abused.

Now that God was older, He enjoyed His irony. He must have. He couldn't help it. It was like the playwright who enjoys the private story note he has written especially knowing his audience cannot.

The old woman waited for her husband to come back from the war. He was a gallant, chivalrous Colonel leading his brave Confederate men to defend their way of life. He had been gone too long. In fact, they had hidden out together in their remote plantation awaiting the end of the war. They had lost the plantation and her husband had died. Her remembrances were the pure fabrication of her mind lost to its denial. Abuses and disappointments of the past had been long forgiven, or at least forgotten as though they had never happened.

Wordlessly, Hanna listened to the woman's fantasy remembrances. She couldn't know her past or the truth of it, but she knew the woman had been powerful once before she had lost all her material things. She had fallen from power but had not known grace. Without that, she had no hope and so lost her mind as well.

Her shining eyes stared away at the distance, at nothing. She spoke without remembering, knowing nothing about Charleston or Savannah or the backland of the Mississippi delta, couldn't know what she didn't know, dreaming every day, some romantic notion, her reality, what she would have wished her life to be, her own selfish picture made up in her own head as her own self-preservation, protecting from the harsh truth of what her life had been, the mind preserving her dignity without her even knowing that either. She didn't know who she was or who Hanna was or what she represented. She had denied herself the salvation of grace and the sanity of hope.

Hanna understood these things and listened. When at last the old woman paused, she took the woman's hands. With her palms turned down and the woman's turned up, Hanna bowed her head and closed her eyes. She rubbed her thumbs in gentle circles in the woman's palms and the woman became calm and quiet and at peace.

Hanna came back often and looked after the woman until the woman passed away. If nothing else, Hanna helped the town folks understand. The woman had shut the world out, except for Hanna.

And they shut the woman out too. She had been a monument to things past, painfully reminding them of lost glory, the way life used to be for them, for everyone who believed in the cause. But she was a burden, a heavy load they could not carry. Best to look the other way and forget.

With their curiosity satisfied, they had no need to come to her funeral. Hanna took care of that too.

Thirteen – Ashford Reunion

They drove their carriage the short half mile south of McComb to Nora Travers's place. David and Josie were not surprised to see how run down the old gray weathered shack appeared.

When they pulled up in the yard, the old woman came out to see who was coming. She looked very old, wrinkled, stooped over, maybe a little crazy, and wary of strangers coming to her place. She was holding a long stick, like a walking staff or a spear with no tip.

"Who yo' folks 'n' wha' does yo' wants heah?"

Josie stepping down from the carriage, said, "Good morning. We heard good things about you in town."

Nora became more relaxed and said, "Good ta heah dat."

"We learned you make potions to make sick folks better", Josie continued.

"Dat's right. Ah does".

David felt Nora was comfortable enough with them and decided to tell her their purpose.

"We are here looking for our sister, Hanna Drish. We heard she lives with you."

"My stars, she do", Nora exclaimed.

"We have been traveling all over Alabama and Mississippi to find her. We've never met her but she is our older sister. We have the same father", David explained.

The old woman beamed and broke out into a broad smile.

She looked like a different woman and said, "Come in da house den. She in tha kichin. We's havin' sum tea."

They looked at each other in wonder and followed old Nora into the house. There, sitting at the kitchen table with her saucer of tea was their sister, a middle aged black woman of large stature, her lined face full of an expression of resolve. In front of her was her bible, opened to Corinthians.

Josie gasped and blurted out, "You look just like our father."

Hanna looked at them puzzled and bemused. She wasn't wary or suspicious, just puzzled.

"You folks sound like Yankees. Hits been a long time since Ah heah da refine' talk ov da educated rich whites or da Yankees."

Josie offered, "We can imagine that. You left the Blanchards in Mobile years ago, didn't you?"

Hanna was confused and wondered how these strangers could know that.

David said, "Hanna, we are your brother and sister. Josiah is our father and yours as well."

She stiffened and looked at them dumbstruck. It had been a long time since she heard her father's name. Suddenly she remembered Mobile and the Blanchards and shifted her manner of speech.

"What are your names? Where do you live? Tell me about my father."

Josie smiled warmly and offered, "Well Hanna Drish, we are from Ohio. Our father lives there and has a furniture factory. Our mother's name is Mary. We were born there thirteen years after you. I am named Josena, after Father's first wife, your mother."

Tears poured down Hanna's cheeks. Her eyes shined. She had so many questions. Nora watched and listened. God was pleased. It was time Hanna found some happiness for herself.

Hanna's head was swimming. She had never given up on finding her father, but now it had come to her so fast and all at once. She struggled to grasp all she was learning.

They spent the whole of the day there together, talking and getting to know each other. The Ashfords agreed to stay in McComb for a while and be with their sister. Eventually they convinced Hanna to leave her settled life, and her mission, and come north for an extended visit, or maybe more.

When they had first arrived in town, they located the one boardinghouse with rooms available for visitors. They found it easily and saw the sign on the front door as they approached to go in. They went in anyway and inquired with the matron at the makeshift front desk in the living room.

"Sorry this is for whites only – no coloreds", she informed them.

"Ya'll can check at tha general storeah. See if they kin hep ya", she offered.

Exasperated, they followed her kind advice and learned there that there was a colored family that took in visitors to town.

With the money the colored family took in from its boarders, they were able to put on a better meal than they would have had on their own. These were hard times in the country, especially for folks like them.

David and Josie got all they could eat of barbeque pork, collard greens, rice with black beans and cornbread. Chicory was the best they could do for coffee. It was a feast and nobody left the table hungry.

The patron had the duty of the supper prayer and told them after, "Hopes ta sees ya'all in church Sunday."

David and Josie said they'd be pleased to come.

"Yankees are Christians too", they told him.

The matron said, "We's all American Christians in ouh country, sum mo' faithful than othas. We's all sinners too, buts we trys ta respec' tha Lord's commandments."

They stayed in McComb several days – visiting Hanna and Nora, sleeping in town in the colored family's home.

Hanna said, "Come wid me ta town wheah Ah works 'n' see ma friens."

She introduced them to the plain folk that were her community.

"Dis heah ma brothah 'n' sistah. They's Yankees from tha North buts still good people."

One Saturday she said, "Now ya come ta church wid me tomorra."

Josie and David smiling said, "Course we will big sister."

Hanna got up and spoke to the congregation that Sunday at her AME church as she did most Sundays during sharing time.

“Ah blessed ta have found ma brothah and sistah”, she told them.

“They’s wid me taday. Gives dem a warm southurn greetin’.”

David and Josie were touched by the welcoming smiles from the congregants. They were with their own people.

“They’s fixin’ ta stay a while”, she added.

“They’s be ovah ta Bessie Johnson’s place til she decides ta throw dem out. So if’n ya’all sees dem roun’, give dem ya best southurn comfort – yo spirit not da whiskey.”

The congregation laughed out loud all at once as one.

Josie leaned over and whispered to David, “And their best southern humor.”

He looked at her and burst out loud laughing.

“Let’s raise ouh hans togethah ‘n’ sing *What a Friend We Have in Jesus*. Calpurnia please lead us in praise.”

‘Hanna is happy here’, David thought. ‘Will she want to come back with us?’, he wondered soberly. ‘Ours is a different world.’

‘We must be together. Hope she sees it that way too’, he concluded.

After the long service was over, they held an informal, plain folks, reception for the Ashfords in the church yard. Mostly it was just lemonade and animated conversation for the whole of the afternoon. The congregation was curious about the northerners and had many questions.

Southerners have to know more about new people whether they be stranger or kin. They are curious and want to spend time asking questions to get acquainted.

Regardless of class or race, they need to know where you are from and who your people are. The reason and root of this is uncertain. Maybe it is a sense of family or interest in the land and places. Maybe it is a protective paranoia from fear of invasion – a closed view of protecting their own – from outsiders or a sense of guilt or inferiority or shame. Maybe it is just a view of country people everywhere – something city people don't know, care about or have time for – a difference in the pace of life. But it is always there and strangers must respond to it when the cultures clash.

So the church members had good conversation with Josena and David. The twins didn't think of it as being nosy. But they wanted to tell them about Hanna too – how much they loved her, how much she meant, how much she had done for their families, their wives and their husbands, children and old folks. She was a Christian inspiration to McComb the eight years she had lived there with them. She was a Christian who walked the walk and had the kindest and most generous heart. She was a Christian pillar and institution.

After she agreed, when she finally decided, to go north with her siblings, David made some preparations. He appeared before the three women at Nora's place one day in his old work clothes he had brought along on the trip.

Hanna asked him, "Wha' ya doin' Yankee brotha'? Are ya tryin' be like us?"

"No", he laughed. "I've got some things to do."

He bought an old buckboard with a broken axle and wheel. He sold the carriage and set about to repair the buckboard and make some modifications. He fixed it up in good running order and built an extended bed with new planks he had fashioned. He added some storage shelves secured for travel and a third seat so that each would have a comfortable place to sit for the long ride.

When they saw what he had done they understood what he had been up to and appreciated his ingenuity.

Just before the day they were to depart, David announced he had one more thing to do. It was a surprise.

"I'll be back later this afternoon", he told them as he shook the reins on the old horse and charged out of Nora's property in a cloud of dust in his new wagon.

While they were waiting for him, the three women sat in Nora's kitchen talking and enjoying cups of chamomile tea. Josie noticed an old fiddle in the corner of the room.

"Nora, do you play that old fiddle?" she asked.

"Ah does onct in a while", Nora answered.

"Mind if I try to play a tune?" Josie asked.

"Course not. Go 'head."

Josie picked up the old relic, held it close to her ear and plucked the strings. She turned the thumbscrews to tighten them into perfect pitch.

"Got a bow?" she asked.

Nora looked in her bedroom and brought her out the bow.

Josie smiled at Nora and said, "See if you know this one".

She warmed up with a slow soft rendition of *Brahm's Lullaby*.

Hanna and Nora's mouths fell open.

She played a lively version of *My Old Kentucky Home* and a deeply heartfelt *Amazing Grace*. Hanna asked how she had ever learned to play like that.

"I have been playing since I was little and I studied violin at university. My college started out as a music school for colored students."

The women smiled at each other, impressed with Josie's hidden talent.

David came back later with a pile of wood in the bed of the wagon. The three women watched him arriving in another cloud of dust.

"Wha' ya got?" asked Hanna.

David smiled at them and proudly declared, "It's dissembled to lay flat for the trip and I know you can't recognize it. It's Father's old pecan kitchen table from Savannah Oaks. We're taking it home to him."

Hanna hadn't seen it in the old plantation when she was there and didn't know what it was. The day she was there, she hadn't gone inside.

David told her, "It will be a surprise for our father. You will see."

They hadn't wanted to tell their father about bringing her home to Ohio until they were sure she would come. They hadn't wanted to tell him they had found her but she wouldn't be coming north either. That would have compelled him to come to Mississippi to see her and he was too old for that. It had worked out for the best as it often does – God's providence solving life's dilemmas.

Fourteen – Going Home

They left on a beautiful summer morning late in June of 1900. Hanna said goodbye to Nora and admonished her to continue their work.

"Now ya look afta' our patiens ole girl. Ya git out mo' 'n' go sees 'em. They's depen' on us ta take care of dem. Our people need ya mo' wid me away. I be gone a long time."

That was the last Nora and Hanna ever saw each other. But they would remember each other fondly.

David told Hanna, "You'll be seeing parts of America you never saw before. We'll be traveling north, following along most of the route Papa traveled with his old friend David, who I'm named after, back in the fall of 1865. I think you'll like it."

Hanna asked if they could visit the Drish plantation. David apologized for it to her – saying it was hundreds of miles out of the way. He explained to her that the trip home would not swing east, but go directly north up the Mississippi to Tennessee, Kentucky and Ohio. While they had covered Josiah and David's trip in reverse, this leg with Hanna was direct and differed somewhat from the old route.

But Hanna saw the regions and land traveled in the past by Josiah Ashford and David Wexley - from Natchez north along the Mississippi River to Tennessee, continuing north to Kentucky, east along the Ohio River to Covington, Kentucky, and finally across the river through Cincinnati to Hamilton, Ohio. For her, of course, the North had a different flavor.

David telegraphed ahead: *Papa, arriving home Monday with our sister Hanna. Stop.*

Josiah and Mary watched for them and were out in the front yard when they heard the carriage arriving.

"Here is your daughter Papa", David told him.

"Hanna, this is our father."

"Hanna, it has been half a lifetime waiting for you my dear girl. Come here and hold me."

"Papa, I never gave up waiting for this day. I never forgot you. All the years I prayed for you."

"God has blessed us both", he said.

The family stood there in the yard for this extraordinary moment, as tears were shed all the way around. It was a monumental reunion, half a lifetime in the making.

Mary's heart melted as she watched them there together.

"Come with me Hanna. I want to show you the room we have begun to prepare for you. It's on the second floor", she said.

"Joe and I moved our bedroom to the main floor a couple years ago, now that we are getting older."

Hanna said, "Thank you for your kindness. What shall I call you?"

"Whatever suits you. Think of me as your old mother. Mama Mary if you like."

Hanna smiled and followed her up the stairs. In the big room they had placed a new Ashford Furniture bed and dresser.

"We can work together on the rest of it after you settle your things. Josie's room is the one next to yours. She is gone a lot but still lives with us."

There seemed to be an understanding that this was not going to be a prolonged visit. The expectation was that she would live here from now on. That evening they had their first family meal together in the formal dining room seated around the majestic mahogany table.

After dinner, Josie brought her violin to the dining room. She explained to Hanna that it was an American-made Guarneri model made by George Gemunder in Astoria New York. It was only a few years old and was beautiful to the eye.

"I'd like to play this to welcome you to the family", she said as she raised it to her shoulder and tilted her neck to its base.

With her arm held perfectly parallel and the bow poised over the strings, she attacked Mozart's Concerto No. 5 in A major, the second movement. It was breathtaking.

"My word", Hanna said. "I'se nevah heard anythin' like dat."

"Thank you Hanna. I wanted you to hear some real fiddle playing."

Not certain of the family protocol in their home and trying to be respectful and mannerly, Hanna asked, "What should I call 'ya Josena".

Josie laughed and said, “You can call me little sister if you want. You have earned the right. I don’t permit David to do that anymore.”

“But you’s twins, da same age.”

“I know, but he has this strange notion that since he was born five minutes earlier than me, he is my big brother.”

Hanna laughed, “Don’t ya worry little sister. Us girls, we stick togetha.”

David said, “Well if you are both through, I’d like to show you around the rest of the house Hanna.”

She smiled and said, “That be fine little brotha.”

David rolled his eyes and led her out of the dining room along the foyer to Josiah’s study. He took her into the room and showed her his big mahogany desk and all the bookcases filled with his books around the room.

“Hanna, Papa accumulated a lot of books in his life. Most of them are his law books from his career in Ohio government.

David Wexley was Papa’s best friend. He wasn’t a master furniture maker and cabinetmaker like our father. He was a master carpenter. But they always worked together and he helped Papa build all these bookcases. I’ll tell you more about our Uncle David after a while. Wait ‘til you see all the machines he invented in the factory for Father’s furniture business. He was an extraordinary white man and part of our family.”

Among other things, he explained to her, it was the curiosity about the Union soldier, David Wexley that led David Ashford to study history. He needed to gain a better understanding of how it was – make it live again in his mind.

After Hanna had been with the family a few days, Josiah asked her to come with him for the day.

"Hanna, let's take a carriage ride. I'd like to spend the day with you, show you around and talk to you. Most of all, I want us to get to know each other."

"That would be so fine, Papa. Me too", she said.

They rode out toward the factory and Josiah told her, "You should have seen this when we first came here. David Wexley and I raised a few dollars doing carpentry for the folks in the area and I bought the old farm here. We started Ashford Furniture in an old barn."

Hanna looked at his face – into his eyes - and said, "I heard so much about Mister Wexley. He meant so much to you didn't he?"

"He did. With his help we built a new life here. More than that, he saved me from drowning in despair when we found your mother had died."

"It must have been a very sad time for you Papa. But I see that God brought you through your trials along with your friend David."

"He did and still does my girl."

He showed her around the bustling factory and she looked in wonder at the activity and size of its operation.

"This is amazin' Papa. All this is yours?"

"Yes, it belongs to our family. That includes you now Hanna."

He drove up the hill to the saw mill and stopped the carriage there. No one was around that time of day.

He turned to her and looking into her eyes said, "No one has said this yet, but I'd like you to live with us from now on. I lost your mother, but I never want to lose you now that you are found."

"I have been thinkin' 'bout my life in Mississippi and the people I tended to there. It will be hard to leave them behind and I will miss them dearly. But I want to be with you and my family now. I have longed for you for so many years of my life. I can't leave you now."

He reassured her, "You can find people here to care for in this community. Your mission can continue. You'll get to know them from our church. There are good people that go to the other church too – some good white people."

She smiled and said, "I have loved the good white people I have found – just as I do our own - just as the Lord taught me to."

Smiling back he said, "I wanted us to have this private day together so that I could tell you about your mother and our life together."

"I have heard 'bout some of it from her when I was a little girl."

"Yes. It was so long ago." He paused, stared away toward the distance thoughtfully, and then added, "But just yesterday".

"We only had two years together. The master – Marcus Taylor married us and she lived with me in my cabin nights and worked in the main house as a servant during the day. One day he took her away and sold her."

"Why did he do it?" she asked as tears began to form in her eyes.

Josiah's eyes began to well up too when he asked, "Are you sure you want to hear the whole story? It is painful?"

"Yes, I need the answers I have waited to hear."

"All right then, I'm going to give you the plain cruel truth. The master, Marcus Taylor bought a slave named Sarah at the Natchez auction when he first built the plantation. He raped her and she gave birth to your mother, Josena. They are your grandparents.

Josena was raised in the planation mansion and the mistress, Rebecca Taylor hated her because of her husband's vile repeated acts with Sarah and because he showed love and affection for Josena and cared for her in the house."

"Wait stop, Papa", Hanna gasped. "I know that Rebecca. I cared for her as a crazy old woman in McComb. I didn't know who she was and she didn't know me either. She made a lot of nonsense talk I couldn't figure out. But she did say her name was Rebecca Taylor."

"That was many years later of course – after the war ended and the plantation fell to ruin", he concluded. "She was always cruel to your mother. She took out all her hate for her husband on his daughter. And Josena was my wife."

"But what you should know is that he sold your mother away when she was grown up and married to me as a young woman. He decided to rid her from his life. It was so that his wife might stop fighting him about it. Her presence every day, and the things he had done, were ruining their marriage".

Hanna began to cry and sobbed, "But how could a father do that?"

Josiah was crying too and said, "My wife was taken away from me at the Savannah Oaks plantation. I didn't know where she went until later, when I found out she had a baby girl soon after coming to the Drish plantation. We both know she was killed there later."

Hanna's eyes were red and brimming with tears.

She said, "I know the rest Papa. Mister Drish cared for her until she died. He brought me to Mister Blanchard for my safety when the war came too close to him. But now Papa – now at last – at long last – God had delivered me to you and we are together."

He was silent for a long moment and throwing his arms around her said, "Now we are together forever."

After their emotions subsided, Josiah drove the carriage back to their house and they joined the rest of the family.

Two days later David Wexley's casket arrived on the train in Cincinnati from Aspen, Colorado. Josiah had explained to his children what had happened with the mining accident out west. David and Josena remembered him fondly as their Uncle David during their childhood years. Hanna was so heartened to see the love between these two great men of different races so long ago after the great Civil War.

Josiah wisely explained to his family again, this time for Hanna's benefit, the way it was this way, "After the war, David Wexley was never content – never satisfied, never happy. He liked people well enough and had a passion for justice. The problem was himself – inside himself.

David had seen too many men exploded by cannon, torn apart by muskets. Those that survived it could never be the same – never right again. Those that didn't experience it, could never know what it was like.

So he kept wandering and searching. He was working as a structural engineer at a silver mine out west in Colorado. There was a planned explosion that went badly and trapped workers inside. He rushed into the tunnel and got killed by a second cave-in from the aftershock."

As an afterthought Josiah reflected that David had written him several times the eight years he was out there. His words presented a brave front, but were dark and sad between the lines.

David hid the table from his father. He worked on it in an abandoned room in the factory, once used for hand finishing of furniture. In this quiet remote corner of the original building, he assembled the old pecan wooden table and cleaned off the decades of grime with turpentine. He hand sanded it with fine grit and rubbed in linseed oil until it shined like gold.

When he brought old Josiah in to see it, he told him, "This was the table you made for the kitchen in Savannah Oaks, Papa. Do you remember?"

Josiah looked at its gleaming finish, the rich pecan with its subtle beautiful straight grain, and the deep beauty marks of character from a generation of slaves preparing food to serve the Massa and the Mistress. He remembered that they gathered around it to eat their own meals together there – all the household women servants, laundresses and attendants, and the male butler and livery man too.

He stood silently looking at its rich gleaming surfaces and sturdy legs- running his hands over it and touching the marks of character stored in its memory and he remembered. He remembered Josena and when he was a young buck full of fire and promise of emancipation and a life better for him and his own.

He smiled through tears of remembrance and said, "Thank you for this gift son. You can never know what it means to me."

David choked up too, said, "We'll put it in the showroom of Ashford Furniture as your first fine piece. It is history, Papa."

They embraced silently for a moment.

Hanna had a few years to spend with her father. Of all her family - her kin now - he was the one she could share a spiritual connection with.

He told her, "I know God has a plan for all of us. He has blessed me."

She knew he had lived all his long life believing that – and what a life it had been, rising above slavery, persevering, enduring and making a difference with it. She adored him for that and understood him better than the others did.

“Father”, she said, “we have lived very similar lives. We have been blessed”.

But she had more to tell him. It was about her life-long secret.

“Papa, I has sumthin ta tell ya. I nevah told nobody ‘bout this bafor”, she said.

He looked at her with the mystery of curiosity and lack of understanding in his warm eyes and told her, “You can tell me. If it is something bad, I will keep your secret.”

“No it wasn’t that. When I was a young girl, livin’ with Ken and Abigail, somthin’ amazin’ happened one night. I was in my room sleepin’ and thought I was dreamin’. God sent his angel Michael to me. I swear He did. He was so big and powerful, at first I was scared. But I felt his love right away and knew it was all right. He told me God had picked me out and His plan for my life.”

His mouth fell open. He looked into her eyes and saw the sincerity.

“What happened? What was it?” he asked.

“He said I would nevah marry or have a family of my own. He wanted me to carry out a special mission fo’ Him all the days of my life. It was more than worshipin’ and believin’ in Him.”

“What was it?”

The tears flowed from her eyes when she said it at last, “He wanted me to bring together the white people and black people I meet in this world. Harmony between them was what God was longin’ fo. I think His heart was brokin’ seein’ all the hate and killin’ goin’ on in the world.”

He realized she had spent her life doing that.

"I believe you my girl. And I see it in you. It is real and I love you."

"He didn't tell me how to do it. I jus' undastood I have ta learn it myself as I go along."

"And you have Hanna. You figured it out better than most of us. Sometimes, rarely, it happens naturally. Remember the improbable friendship I had so long with David Wexley – a white man from Baltimore, a Union soldier I met after the war. We were brothers Hanna. He taught me what was possible."

She knew that it was.

"He came to me agin' papa. It was on the road when I was walkin's 'cross Mississippi. He lifted me up when I was down. He gave me the power of touch fo' healin'", she said.

When at last she was finished, they sat together looking across the fields from their porch. It was warm but the air was dry. The Ohio sun made the brown grasses glisten like gold. He held her hand and wondered.

Years later, when he was older and sick, she touched him and he felt it. He understood and believed then for certain.

He had a very special love for her.

She took it real hard when he passed away.

Fifteen – To Everything There Is a Season

And a time to every purpose under heaven

A time to be born, a time to die
A time to plant, a time to reap
A time to kill, a time to heal
A time to laugh, a time to weep

A time to build up, a time to break down
A time to dance, a time to mourn
A time to cast away stones, a time to gather stones together

A time of love, a time of hate
A time of war, a time of peace
A time you embrace, a time to refrain from embraces

A time to gain, a time to lose
A time to rend, a time to sew

The legislature up in Columbus was not in session, so Josiah had been around home. He had been slowing down anyway.

He got up one morning and had breakfast with Mary. As old folks do, they reminisced about the children growing up and how much life was changing in the modern age.

He was restless and told her, "Mary, I'm gonna go over to the factory and poke around a bit. I'll be back before noon."

"Don't stick your nose in where it's not needed dear."

He smiled and went upstairs to dress for the day. He put on his favorite white linen shirt without a collar, and open in the front, and his baggy comfortable slacks and left for the short walk to the end of his property. He looked up at how big the factory had become. It had certainly taken on a life of its own in recent years. He felt more apart from it.

He located his superintendent and asked him how business was going.

Frank, uncomfortable with the boss's question, had to admit, "Production has slowed down and inventory is up because sales have been fallin' off the past two months."

"I want to have a meeting with the department heads and talk about this. Would you gather them together in the conference room right now?"

"Sure Josiah. Give us about fifteen minutes."

He nodded and walked around the production floor to observe the workers and their output. He looked at the raw stock inventory, the finishing rooms and the finished goods staged for delivery.

When the meeting was convened, Josiah looked around at them from the head of the big table with his stern expression of resolve, this time maybe more sinister, and asked, "What's going on? What's happened to sales?"

David and Josena were not present.

There was a silent pause until the head of sales spoke up, "As you know the economy is not good and we've about saturated the market in our region."

Josiah put his hand to his chin and postulated, "By now I would have expected we would have increased our reach beyond Ohio to New York, Michigan, Indiana and Kentucky."

"You know we have been selling into Kentucky for years boss."

"Well I want something done about it. This is not acceptable", he said as he got up and left the room.

He was concerned and couldn't stop thinking about it. That evening he found David, met him in the study and told him about the meeting. David listened attentively and respectfully. He had heard about this himself.

"Papa, maybe it's time you stepped down and let me take over. You've got enough to do around here."

Josiah glared at him and said, "What enough? You think I'm too old to run my own company?"

"No of course not. I'm just suggesting maybe Josie and I have more energy to carry on the fight."

Josiah remained silent for so long David began to wonder what the old man was thinking or whether he was thinking at all.

Finally, Josiah got up abruptly from his comfortable leather chair in the study and said, "Well all right then. I will step down and the next generation can take over."

"We will always come to you for advice Father."

He smiled and said, "You'd better boy, if you know what's good for you."

The end of an age had come.

Shortly before he died, while his intelligence was still at its full capacity, Josiah Ashford gave his last speech. It was a private one for his family.

They were gathered in the big kitchen of the estate for the family reunion when he said:

"History is a tragedy, not a morality tale. It is a record of what happened because of what some men did.

God knows this is true. Because He is eternal, His clock runs on a different scale than mans'. What for us is scores of years, is seconds to Him. He knows what I have always said to you, and you have now learned for yourselves to be true. That is, that man is a combination of goodness and evil.

Man is most often motivated by his self- interest. It is rare that he is self-sacrificing. All we can do is seek out the goodness in ourselves and in others to strive to make life better for as many as we can. You have all seen and done this as well. For that, you know I am proud of all of you. Hanna's life is a sterling example of that motive. Her life proves there is divine intervention.

But it is rare that God intervenes anymore, like he did in monumental ways at the beginning of His creation. He had decided to give us free will and knows the consequences of that better than any of us ever can.

Only now He has decided to act in more gentle and softer ways. He has made some of man His instruments and placed them among us. Some have seen His signs and others have no knowledge of the purpose He has placed within them.

All that we can do is what we have always known – act justly and show mercy."

Mary had been watching his eyes and smiling said, "Joe, you should have been called Peter. Like Simon called Peter, you have been the rock of this church."

Josena looked at her mother and said, "God knows that's true Mama."

Josiah laughed and looking at Mary said, "You have always been so smart and now you are wise. Only God knows how you can still be so beautiful at seventy four."

David reflected and thought out loud, "It's true what he said about the perspective of the span of time. He was born a slave in 1829 in Missouri. Now he is a respected, revered and successful old man here in Hamilton, Ohio in 1905."

He had been thinking, 'Just 30 miles north of here Orville and Wilbur Wright are inventing and building experimental flying machines in their bicycle shop. There are conducting tests flights there on Huffman Prairie and in North Carolina. Just in the span of one man's lifetime.'

Hanna looked at all of them and said, "God has blessed us all for our family."

Josiah woke up one morning in the spring of 1906 with a desire to look at his land. He went outside where the air was fresh and the temperature was beginning to rise from the early sun's warmth. He walked over to his barn but decided not to drive his new Ford motor car.

Instead he saddled up his prized white stallion, put his foot in the stirrup and swung onto his back. He galloped out of the barn and across the yard. Along the road, as he came to his sawmill, he slowed down and decided to stop.

He dismounted and walked over to a pile of fresh cut maple planks. As he bent down to pick one up and look down its edge to see how flat and straight it was, he smiled when he remembered he and Ned doing this all those years ago on Savannah Oaks plantation.

He winced as he felt a sharp pain in his arm. With a shortness of breath he sat down on the ground. The blue sky grew dark to his vision as he passed out, drawing his last breath.

It was quiet there that beautiful morning. His horse nickered, knowing something was terribly wrong. When his sawmill attendant heard this, he came over and found him dead.

What good fortune the family had been there all together to bury him in the family cemetery and memorialize his life.

For reassurance to the Ashfords, the minister had said, "May He support us all, till the shades lengthen, and the evening comes, and the busy world is hushed, and the fever of life is over, and our work is done. Then in His mercy may He give us a safe lodging, and a holy rest, and peace at last."

After the funeral, Mary was like a ship without a rudder. She spent long days daydreaming on the porch looking out over the fields. Her memories were more sweet than bittersweet.

Hanna became her companion and kept her connected to this world for the last years of Mary's life. During their long afternoons together at the Ashford house, Mary told Hanna about her long life and family history as though she was talking about a life that was finished.

"Hanna, my life was very different from yours and your father's. Martha Washington, George Washington's wife, kept her slaves until President Washington died.

They were called dowry slaves. That was because she was given them from her family when she married him and they belonged to her. Since they were her property, she decided to keep them until after old George died. We were all named Custis because that was Martha's family name.

She freed them shortly after his death in 1799. Many of us left to come west to Ohio here. It's been three generations we have been freeborn since then. I am the fourth.

Mary wanted Hanna to understand something about slavery that Hanna might never have known.

She said, "We all think about President Lincoln with love and gratitude because he freed the slaves. It's true he believed in abolition but he didn't believe we were equal. He wondered how we would get along in life on our own. He thought it might be better if we were sent back to Africa."

Hanna's mouth fell open in disbelief.

"There is much people in the north don't know about the South", she continued. "Before George Washington was President, he gave up his comfortable life and sacrificed everything for his country – he led us in the Revolutionary War."

"I knows that", Hanna said.

"He had a slave – a personal servant – who was with him through all the troubled times. The man was loyal and believed in him even though George owned him as property. He was a Custis like all my people. George talked to him more about things sometimes than he did white men. There was an abiding affection – an intimacy - between them based on their constant companionship. My ancestor loved him. When George died, he grieved for him like he would his own kin. People don't know about that, or if they do, don't understand it."

Hanna listened attentively, then said, "That may be true Mary, but I know how colored people were treated in the South. I have seen it and lived it. The cruelty of white people who call themselves Christians and the way they acted toward other human beings was a sin God will surely punish them for."

Mary shook her head in agreement and said, "I'm certain that is true too and I don't want to minimize your father's suffering. Believe me, I have seen the scars on his back."

Mary continued, "When I first met your father, he was a freedman. That's different than a freeborn person. It means he once was a slave, whereas my ancestors and I never were. We always felt somehow we were superior to the former slaves because of that.

But I saw great qualities in your father. His spirit and gift of looking to the future made him exceptional to all the notions we might have had."

Hanna had seen this herself and replied, "I know that's true Mama Mary. I thank the Lord I got to know him finally at the end of his life."

They sat quietly together and reflected on their conversation.

Later, after Mary died too, Hanna still yearned to know about the early life of her mother and father on the Mississippi plantation. She went to David to see what he could tell her. She told him she had heard about the tragedies and the hardships, but she wanted to know about the happiness.

David looked at her sympathetically and told her, "The stories from father and his friend David are full of their struggles. Unfortunately, that is what has been told the most."

"I knows it", she said. "Papa told me all that, but just said they were in love and married a short time. Mama Mary talks 'bout papa's success and hows he rose up here in Ohio in his new life."

He tried to help her understand and said, "Father didn't keep a diary or write letters. He wasn't much for looking back. With him and David and your mother gone, there's parts of the story we will never know. Sometimes it happens that way. All the things we long to know from the past, we can't get once the generation has left us."

"All I know is that they were deeply in love and helped each other all they could in their troubled times", he said. "Maybe that is enough for us now", he added with resignation.

"I 'spose it is. I know my mamma was a wonderful mother to me in Alabama befor' she was killed. I kin still remembah that."

"And father never gave up looking for her until he learned the horrible truth and lost you for so long", he added.

"But de Lord brought us together in the end David. Thass the mos' important thing."

When David Ashford finally came to the decision to take over management of Ashford Furniture in earnest, he began to find out a lot of things about its corporate rot that had led to its decline and could have led to its demise.

He asked his sister to help him and Josie did all she could with the time she had available. More importantly, she was his sounding board when he needed one. They were both very intelligent and had always sounded each other out since they were children. They were twins and nearly alter egos.

First he learned what he always thought to be true – that Frank, a large, beefy, affable white man that had been with Josiah since manufacturing had first taken on a true factory operation, was a good man. He was honest and loyal and always looked out for the best interests of the company. He had a steady hand running the everyday operation of all aspects of the production. David liked him and knew he could count on him.

When David closely examined the company ledgers, he found some discrepancies. Some money had gone missing. He traced it carefully and found out the bookkeeper, a sour, unpleasant black man Josiah had cultivated from the ranks, had been slowly absconding with small amounts of money for over a year.

He called him into his office and told him exactly to the penny how much he had taken. He reckoned his back pay and severance wouldn't cover it, so he kept it and sent the man packing that day. David kept the books himself for three months until he found a reliable man, a Yankee from Philadelphia, to take over.

He fired the sales manager who had been resting on the laurels of his former glory, taking kickbacks from the owners of the retail store outlets he had been selling to, and not getting out with the sales reps to find new channels of distribution. He hired a seasoned salesman who had been a graduate of Miami of Ohio business school, specializing in marketing. Within a year the company had begun to turn around.

He sat in his office, feet on the desk, looking out the window at their house across the field and thought, 'I'm glad Father never lived to see this. He would have been so disappointed after all he did to build the company. At least Frank has maintained the quality. That was always the source of Papa's pride.'

He was also thinking about the many homes and stores that had emerged for the families that were dependent on his furniture company. The hamlet of Ashford, Ohio was a part of it. It had become an integrated community where the races lived together in relative peace and harmony.

He had an inherited responsibility to all those people for their livelihood and sustenance. He had not let them down.

Josena had remembered the satisfaction she had experienced from teaching. She had taught children – mostly girls – how to play the violin. When one or two of them excelled, it was a joy and a fulfillment. Now she was a doctor of philosophy in sociology, anthropology and archeology.

She had spent all her youth mastering her knowledge and never married. She had studied, traveled, written a book. Now it was time to teach what she knew to the eager college students. She knew there would be a few that would embrace it and it would set their lives on a path.

So Josena began teaching at university. She befriended a younger associate professor of history, Elizabeth Jefferson – a white woman. Her friends called her Peggy.

Her family had moved to Hamilton from New York during the Depression of 1893 when her father, Sam Jefferson had sought work. He found it in the Ashford Furniture Company and rose from a laborer to a highly skilled craftsman.

As Josena and Peggy became more inseparable, Josie brought her home and introduced her to the family. They had a family dinner and David was quite taken with Peggy's looks and perky personality.

She was a surprise for him. He had known Sam from the factory for years but never learned much about his family. He didn't know Sam had such a fetching daughter. He became more interested when he learned she was a history professor.

When he called on her at her home, it was awkward for many reasons. Sam was surprised to find that David was interested in his daughter.

"This might not be a good idea, Mr. Ashford", was all he said.

David asked him why.

He was surprised when Sam told him, "You are so much older than my girl and I work for your family at the factory."

"Oh. Well look it Sam, my passion has always been history and I share that with Peggy. She is so smart and delightful. If you can abide it, I plan to continue seeing her."

"That would be entirely up to you and Peggy. I just think it's not a good idea is all", Sam said.

"Maybe it's because I'm black and there will be trouble", David offered.

Sam frowned and said, "That will be a big problem for some but not me. I'm thinkin' it will be the biggest problem for the two of you."

He knew Sam made sense and couldn't dislike him for his honesty. Still he couldn't help his irritation.

"I'll bear that in mind", he said.

Peggy and David did continue to keep company and they did discuss race. They were determined to face it clear-eyed, head-on and with no recriminations between them. They knew that if they couldn't resolve it conclusively between themselves, they would never be able to stand up to the prejudice that people would throw at them.

David appreciated Peggy's agile mind and soon came to fall in love with her. By that time in the North, miscegenation was not viewed as so sinful as in the South and in the recent past.

On one occasion he told Peggy, "I know racism and slavery are closely related – the former spawned by the latter."

"I think of it as cultural and, of course, societal", she offered. "It's so much about the notions of nobility and class."

David smiled in agreement and added, "When I think about our country, I recall the two groups of English who founded it – so different, the pious New Englanders in Massachusetts and the arrogant Royal Cavaliers in Virginia. They were all Anglicans or at least Protestants. But it is because of their different view about class, the North always tended toward equality and the South became so much like the Old World repeating itself."

"You're right", she said. "I see exactly what you mean. Christianity is all tied up in it for sure. Certainly, in the early history of the mercantile North, there was white indentured servitude and black slavery. But in the South, the planters built a true new England with nobles and their land, their fiefdoms and their peasants. They had no middle class, just the few nobles and the many peasants – black ones they owned and white ones struggling at the bottom."

"I agree with you that that is how it happened. But it is changing. Like the poet might say, 'There is a new day dawning'."

She smiled at him lovingly. David, this black man was 43 and Peggy, this white woman was an energetic 34.

It is a big decision when a couple decides to marry. For David and Peggy, it was momentous. They would be the first mixed union in Butler County, Ohio in 1912 and they knew it. But because it was with the Ashford name, the people there had little choice but to accept it, no matter how begrudgingly. Ashford Furniture Company employed many of them directly or else their independent businesses and farms were directly affected by the manufacturer, usually profoundly. The village of Ashford was a one-horse town.

David had few friends in his own life, mostly just many acquaintances that respected him. So he asked his production manager Frank to be his best man. They liked and respected each other and the bi-racial connection would be important. Frank accepted his role graciously. He has always been loyal to David and Josiah before him. Besides he knew what was in his best interest.

The white people would attend the AME church for the ceremony, and the reception at the Ashford estate afterwards, alongside the black people. Some stayed home and some blacks did too. There were many whites that viewed blacks as inferior. There were many blacks that couldn't abide by the mixing of the races of either gender from the stigma of bitterness going back to slavery.

While Sam Jefferson was for the Union – had fought with Grant's 131st Ohio Infantry in '64 – and for emancipation, it appeared he was not for this union. Like Lincoln, he wasn't convinced the races were equal.

It seemed he wouldn't come to the wedding to give Peggy away to her Negro groom and sit there with his wife. On the day of the ceremony, Sam appeared and carried out his fatherly duty.

If David had not been an Ashford, odds were he wouldn't have come. But he did and walked Peggy down the aisle in the AME church. He didn't have a change of heart. It was a pragmatic decision for his daughter, his wife and his employment.

In the middle of the hard winter of 1915, Peggy delivered a baby boy. They named him Josiah Ashford II. He was coffee colored with bright hazel inquisitive eyes. And he grew to be a handful – smart like his father, energetic like his mother and precocious himself.

Joe was the first mixed race boy in the minds and recollection of the people in the area. But there had been others in the family. Only the direct family – David, Josena, Hanna, Mary – knew that his grandmother Mary was a descendent of freeborn blacks that had come from Martha Custis and George Washington's slaves. They might have been inbred if George or his white people had raped their slaves like Tom Jefferson had. No one knew either way for sure. His father David and aunt Josena might have been of mixed race too because of that lineage. It got complicated in a hurry.

And his step aunt Hanna. She had been born from the slaves Josena and Josiah, Joe's grandfather. But that Josena, a slave girl down in Mississippi, had descended from her mother, the feisty slave girl Sarah and her father, Marcus Taylor who had raped his slave as an act of lustful loneliness, desperate dominance and vile vengeance.

African Americans in the future would make this investigation – this tracing of roots - their life's work. But so often it was only to find sympathy for the black members and pride in their hard brave heritage and to condemn the white members for their evil cruelty. This would be the emphasis that would be taught to them as they achieved their higher education in modern colleges. It was a true harsh reality that needed to be understood, but would do nothing to promote racial harmony. Quite the contrary, it would delay it for the foreseeable future.

God would wish them to remember. It would be an important lesson. But He wanted them to find harmony and peace, despite the hurt of the remembering, the knowing and the understanding. He longed for it. Hanna knew this.

This was the way it was in Ohio, in the early 20th century.

The winds of war began to blow again. This time it was in Europe. In 1914 the Archduke Ferdinand, heir to the throne of the Austro-Hungarian Empire, was assassinated in Sarajevo, the capital of Bosnia. Germany and Russia joined into the dispute between the Empire and Serbia.

President Wilson was determined to remain neutral and keep America out of the fight. He was successful for a while.

Sixteen – War in France

When the Spanish American War broke out in 1898, David was 29 and traveling through the South with Josena to trace the route his father had traveled before. He had been following the national politics and viewed the attack on Cuba as an imperialist act by the United States to remove the last of Spanish influence from the Western Hemisphere. The flamboyant actions by young Teddy Roosevelt were viewed by some as heroic and patriotic.

By then David had seen much of the post- Civil War South and, with his background and passion for history, had decided to become a newspaper correspondent.

The United States joined its allies to participate in World War I in 1917. So in the spring of 1918 when he was 48, David Ashford responded by attaching himself to the U.S. army as a war correspondent. This was late in World War I. President Wilson and the will of the American people had delayed involvement in the European war of German aggression as long as possible. German atrocities at sea had forced the decision to enter the war.

The draft raised nearly three million men. Two million more volunteered. Four hundred thousand African Americans enlisted or were drafted. Fifty thousand went to France. There their units were segregated and they served under white commanders.

When the Selective Service Act was passed in 1917, African American males joined the war effort to prove their loyalty, patriotism and worthiness for equal treatment in American society. In World War I, there were four all-black black regiments – the 9th and 10th cavalry and the 24th and 25th infantry. Only a few got the opportunity to serve in combat units. The 92nd and 93rd Divisions were created as primarily black combat units.

David had nothing to prove to his country about his worthiness as a patriot but joined up with General Jack Pershing's American Expeditionary Force and sailed to France to join the Allies and defend against the German invasion. This was the first time an African American Ashford had been to France or even Europe.

As a war correspondent, he had attended the black officer trainee's camp at Fort De Moines under command of LTC Charles Ballou. He trained along with the regular infantry, was in the top of his group, and was commissioned as a Captain. He observed and fought with the 93nd formed from National Guard units in Ohio and under direct command of BG Roy Hoffman. They fought bravely at the front lines in the Argonne forest.

He had full access to the front line action and reported the events for back home. Standing with the front line commanders, he observed officers as leaders who had to constantly motivate their men to engage in battle and face almost certain death.

He found out that the British and French Allies were worn out from the fighting there that had gone on for three years and had reached a stalemate in the trenches. The Russians had left the fight.

With the impetus of the American forces, the Allies repulsed the German offensive at Chateau-Thierry, just fifty miles from Paris. Shortly after, at Muese-Argonne in the Argonne Forrest, the Americans pushed the Germans back to their border. The Germans sought an armistice before their country was invaded.

For the Americans, the fighting was brief but with heavy casualties. David would spend only eight months there before the war would be over.

He had experienced those moments when he watched across from the trenches the surreal dark moving figures like ghosts in the smoke and the mist, and the moments when the men left the trenches, climbed out of them and formed a charge at the enemy line.

Blindly charging into the blazing machine guns, so many fell instantly and were gone. In that moment, that intense moment of terror and clarity, there was no past or no future, only that brilliant moment in the present. As the consciousness narrowed and focused, there was no fear either any longer. It was replaced with rage and blood lust until it was over.

It was like his father's friend David had said about the Civil War. Not much had changed about men killing men on the grandest scale. Lee had learned from Longstreet about fortification and trench warfare to slow down the rate of the killing.

Chemical warfare was used here on a large scale and the soldiers shrieked with pain as the mustard gas burned their faces and exposed parts of their bodies. Mostly though the casualties in the trenches were from heavy shelling. A "no-man's land" formed a space between the two lines of trenches. But ultimately one or both sides had to move at the enemy. But then once again in World War I, the killing had become even more efficient.

Again the young men who were there would wonder why God would permit it, why he would turn a blind eye to his human beings – his creations – destroying each other for land and resources or for differences in their ideologies.

In the thick of the fighting, from his observation point, David's mind often wandered. He pictured his father's dearest friend David and the stories he had heard about the Civil War.

He now understood what Uncle David had meant when he described it. Now he had learned about it for himself. It would change him for the rest of his life as it had so profoundly changed Uncle David and all soldiers who had served in mortal combat.

With his father and Uncle David gone, he wanted to share his thoughts and experiences with his mother and sisters when this nightmare was finished. His mind steered his memory to his father and he grieved once again.

He was lonely and homesick and grew despondent. He longed to re-unite with his family when this was over. He wanted to hold them all in his arms – his wife and little son, his sister and his mother. Pieces of his heart remained home with them. But the heart grows and is not diminished. It remains intact and lives beside the soul.

Mary passed away in 1917 while David was overseas in France and eleven years after her husband's passing. Hanna had brought her peace in her last years and she died fulfilled with no regrets.

Josena remembered to send word back to Virginia so that the funeral was delayed until the Rev. Bernard W. Custis arrived from there to participate in the ceremony. She met him at the train in Cincinnati and drove him up to Hamilton. The Reverend traced his Custis lineage from Martha's people, but he had known many of the later generation freeborn men and women on the other side of the family that had kept the name.

On the morning of the funeral service he was made welcome in the Ashford family's African Methodist Episcopal Church as kin. The huge chapel was filled to capacity by family, neighbors and the community of both races. Everyone knew Mary and loved her for her grace and soft-spoken kindness. Josena and Hanna sat in the front with Joe between them.

The chapel was warm and noisy with the crowd huddled together there that bright morning. A hush fell over them as the two men walked over to the pulpit.

Their AME pastor looked out at the crowded room, seeing as many white faces as black, and introduced the guest pastor Bernard Custis as a childhood friend of Mary's. He acknowledged the presence of her daughter, step-daughter and little grandson. He mentioned that it was a pity that her son David was overseas and could not be there with them. He opened the service with a prayer of reassurance and stepped aside as Rev. Custis stepped to the pulpit.

The reverend shared his childhood memories of Mary and said, "She always called me Bernie when we grew up together in Fairfax. It was long before the war and a time of peace for us.

Mary was the 3rd freeborn generation tracing back to Martha Custis Washington's slaves. She had let them go free when George died in 1799 in Mount Vernon.

So much has passed before God's eyes since that time. So many trials and tribulations. But today we are together, all God's children, to remember Mary and the gift her life has brought us.

Take a moment to look around at each other. Look into each other's faces and see the shining eyes. God's love is with us. He lives in our hearts. Bless you and may His peace be with you."

As he sat down, the AME pastor nodded to Josena and she rose from her place in the congregation and walked up to the pulpit. The pastors each gave her a brief embrace before she turned toward the people with a small piece of paper in her hand.

She smiled at them and spoke to the guest pastor, "I am so gratified you are here with us today Bernie. It is fitting that you were my mother's first white friend.

These were my father's last words he wrote to my mother before he died:

> *Grieve not for me nor speak of me with tears but laugh and talk of me as though I were beside you – I loved you so it was heaven here with you.*

My mother felt that way about all us here today. She loved us all and she loved our community. She will be dearly missed. But we will remember her with a smile for the time she graced us with her life. Time cannot steal the treasures that we carry in our hearts, nor dim the shining thoughts our cherished past imparts."

She slowly folded the paper and, with her head down, walked backed to her seat next to Joe.

After the congregation joined together in the hymn, *What a Friend We Have in Jesus*, the pastor raised his hands and closed the service with, "God has said, 'Never will I leave you; never will I forsake you.' God bless you and be with you as you face this time of sorrow. And may He give you hope and strength to meet each new tomorrow."

Josena and Hanna buried her in the family cemetery on the Ashford estate. She was placed to rest next to Josiah's plot on his right. David Wexley was buried on Josiah's left.

It was a time of joy – something Christians understand when they bury their dead. The body they put in the ground is just an empty shell of their loved one. They know that the spirit has departed and they rejoice with that promise and solace.

After the armistice was signed, the war was over and David returned from overseas to the States on a military ship. From the port of New York City, he took a train to Cincinnati. He had forwarded a message to the family and they all gathered at the train station to welcome him home. David was excited to see his sisters Josena and Hanna and his wife Peggy and little Joe, now three years old. He noticed right away his mother was missing.

"Where's Mother, Josie", he asked.

"I'm so sorry David. She passed away and we couldn't get word to you. You were in the heat of it and we weren't allowed to contact you", she replied.

"I knew her health was failing, but I'm devastated I missed her funeral."

Hanna said, "After we git you home, we will visit her grave and have a family prayer. She passed peacefully brother. We was with her when her soul was sent to heaven".

"Let's all go home", was all David could say.

Exhausted, he kissed Peggy, scooped up Joe on his shoulder, and Josie and Peggy carried his luggage to the car. They went home.

He did visit his mother's gravesite and grieved for her and his father and David Wexley. He began to feel his own mortality at age forty nine. He was thinking about his little son Joe – Josiah Ashford II.

"Joe never knew his grandfather or David Wexley and he won't remember his grandmother after he is grown up", he told Peggy.

Peggy looked at his crestfallen expression and reassured him, "It is the way of life David. Some leaves fall and others grow in their place. To everything, there is a season."

"I know it. But I've been thinking about writing a book. I need to capture our family history in the context of our American history", he had decided.

He began the book and Josie helped him as his editor. But more than that she helped him to remember – the story of Josiah brought to Savannah Oaks as a slave from Missouri, his wife the first Josena, the cruel Civil War, his devoted friend David, the struggle of the freedmen and poor whites after the killing was over, Ohio, their mother Mary, the discovery of their divinely inspired sister Hanna, The World War and the century of changes in America.

More than a family biography, it traced the origins and path of slavery from Egyptian and Arabic culture in northern Africa to Europe and the British colonies in North America. David wrote about the earliest slaves brought to New Amsterdam by the Dutch and to Virginia for the English tobacco planters.

He wrote about the little-known practice of indentured servitude of white children and white young adults imported to the northern Colonial cities. Poor families in England sold their children to America for a seven-year term contract to pay off their debt, or for money to survive, or for prisoners to fulfill their penalty for their crimes.

Peggy had told him there were also the many poor Irish enslaved in America. The “servants” were worked so hard and treated so harshly, they often died before their terms were completed. They had little opportunity for a better life here.

But David’s message was predominately a positive one, as inspired by his family, from its heroes like his father and David Wexley, and heroines like his sisters and mother. He made sure Hanna’s message of love and hope for humanity’s harmony was not missed.

He spent eight years writing it and finished it in 1926. He entitled it *The Son of a Slave in America* and Random House in New York published it the same year as William Faulkner’s darker view of humanity, *Absalom, Absalom*!, was released. David’s biography was on the best sellers list.

He mailed a copy of his book’s first printing to Professor McPherson at the history department at University of Alabama to give the man more perspective.

Before the war, David had been an infrequent contributing writer to the local newspaper. With his experience in France as a war correspondent, he returned home to the Hamilton-Oxford newspaper as a regular weekly contributing column reporter. He wrote editorial commentary on the news and events in the country from his unique historical and sociological perspective.

America was changing rapidly in the 20’s. He enjoyed discussing these things with his sisters – the advancements in airplanes since the early days of the Wright brothers, the aftermath of the war in Europe, women’s suffrage, the Scopes trial right up in Tennessee, the incredible appreciation in the stock market from speculative investment.

Sometimes he waxed philosophical – said that history took care of its own, that it was in the hand of fate, not men. Hanna disagreed with that and told him it was in God's hands like General Lee had thought – providence. He was impressed that she could think of that example for her perspective. His divinely inspired, older sister from the South and another mother was amazing really – the way she looked at things and considered them.

With her insight, Hanna told David how it was. She said, "David, you knows I grew up in the South wid two while families. I lived da history you talk 'bout. I lived wid dem long after I be freed. They believed in da Confederacy and der cause long after the war was ovah. Da Drishs and da Blanchards, they adjusted to da changes 'bout colored people, but nevah forgot der dreams 'bout der way of life. So I hear all dese stories all dose years 'bout der Generals who was heroes to dem.

They specially love Robert E. Lee and his faith in God. I heard 'bout General Thomas Jackson they call Stonewall too. He used to pray evra night frum de New Testament. Den every day he fight wid da fury of da Old – smiting his enemies mightily as God had commanded. Dat was just how they were and how hit was."

He wrote a newspaper article about Hanna's recollections for his Ohio readers to understand how it was.

Seventeen - Spotted Horse on the Hill

She comes down easy soon after the leaves fall
A spotted filly's hooves coming down the hill in the soft brown earth
Easy-like walking tender over the wet leaves
Cooler and quiet and gentle

The winds blow colder near the bottom of the hill
She struggles harder and the land turns dead
At the bottom dead sticks and gray sky
Clouds moving fast from the west bringing her harder

Snow falling silently all the dark days and nights
Sparkling ice in the bright cold sun
Blurry sad moon waiting long nights for her journey to end

She stumbles and goes on older up the hill
An old mare tired and worn

Her last steps bring her back to the top of the hill
She steps lighter in the warm sun
The land is soft and green again
She is young once more

The winter of 1924 was harsh in Buffalo, New York. Crista Hannon left in the spring with her husband and baby daughter. She was pregnant again and feeling worn but hopeful. Hans was out of work and they were looking for a better life.

They drove west in their old Ford motor car packed with all their belongings. They headed southwest after Cleveland and kept going almost to the Ohio River across from Kentucky. When Hans spotted the large factory, they stopped near the town of Hamilton - just south of it next to the village of Ashford. German migrants like the Hannons joined the African Americans coming from the South there in that rural, hopeful patch of earth.

This had always been the American story for whites and was becoming so for blacks. This was a big country with plenty of room for everybody.

After the war, and as a result, America would be changing again. There would be another "Great Migration" of blacks from the rural South to the northern industrial cities. Seventy thousand went to Chicago from Alabama and Mississippi. Once again, as after the Civil War, blacks sought opportunity in the North. Many came to the Industrial Belt in cities like Cleveland and Detroit for work in the factories. The industrial boom of the war had brought new hope for a better life.

Labor became available throughout rural areas as well. Migrants of both races came to the Hamilton area and some settled in the new town of Ashford. They brought a talent for working with their hands and mechanical skills.

Ashford Furniture Co. had grown under its management and Josena's oversight while David was overseas; but now with the new labor pool available, David brought it to a new level as a major manufacturer in southwest Ohio. He hired a middle management staff who developed programs for training. The raw talent of the labor pool was honed and shaped for the skills needed to make fine furniture.

Hanna took full advantage of the growing Ashford village community to spread her care to its bi-racial residents. As a result of Ashford Furniture's success and growth, the area was developing rapidly with new churches, bars, restaurants, shops, parks and municipal offices. The white migrants moving in from the east and African Americans from the south came to raise their families and for a better life. She cared for the working class people's homes, their children and their health. At last she had a bigger calling than the town of McComb back in Mississippi. And conditions were more modern, not as primitive as that poor southern town.

She met the new arrivals in town. Like a one-woman welcoming committee, she offered to help them settle and adjust, mind their children and heal their illnesses where she could. All this she did in the name of Christianity and friendship.

When she met Hans and Crista Hannon from New York, he was a machinist and a new hire starting work at the furniture company. Crista was six months pregnant with their second child and feeling poorly.

"We haven't known any coloreds in New York", Crista told her.

"But you are nice enough", she said.

"I'm Crista Hannon. What is your name?" she asked.

"I'm Hanna Drish. My brothah David Ashford runs the furniture factory and my sistah Josena teaches at Miami of Ohio."

"But you don't have the same name as your brother and sister", she said.

"I knows dat seem funny. We had the same fathah, Josiah Ashford. I kep the name my owner in Alabama give me."

"So you are part of the family this town is named after?"

"Yes I is. My family owns the factory and I lives with them on the family farm. Hit's a long story how I was found in Mississippi by my brothah an sistah and brought back here to live wid my fathah years ago. Lord sakes, listen to me chatterin' away like a squirrel treed by an ole hown dawg."

Crista laughed, "You are funny."

Hanna told her, "We git along jus' fine onct we git ta know each othah."

Crista smiled and said, "I can see that, and your help is much appreciated, a Godsend really."

Hanna sat with her some days while Hans started his new job.

She came to the Hannon's run-down rented house one early summer day and no one answered the door. She could hear the baby crying and let herself in. Crista was in bed moaning and uncomfortable.

Hanna asked, "How ya doin' today girl?"

"Oh, I'm feeling sick", she said. "The baby's kicking me day and night. I can't sleep and don't want to eat."

"I brought sum chamomile wid me. Let me fix you some tea. It'll hep wid yo stomick and yo digestin. I knows that baby pushin' hard on yer innards."

"Thank you Hanna. I'm feeling poorly and can't wait for this baby to get out."

"It'll be soon I reckon, from the look of you", Hanna reassured her.

"I want to do sumthin' to figure how yo doin' and hep ya'", Hanna offered.

"What is it?"

She laid her two large hands flat and gentle across Crista's swollen belly. She bowed her head and mumbled an inaudible prayer.

"Feel dat?" she asked.

Crista felt an electric tingle all across the middle of her body.

She smiled and said, "I feel better."

"Seems everythin' is right. Ya shud be deliverin', soon", Hanna reassured her.

She delivered their first son two weeks after that and named him Ashford Hannon.

With things more settled, Hanna kept up her friendly visits. Crista's recovery from this second baby was harder. Hanna would take the older child off her hands and out for walks in the village – to the corner store for penny candy. Townsfolk got used to seeing them together and looked forward to it.

She offered to get Crista out more too.

"If hit make ya feel bettah, yo be welcome ta come to church dis Sunday. Ya might like hit if ya wants", she said.

Hanna attended her own AME church most Sundays, but sometimes visited the Baptist and Presbyterian churches the white people attended. She wanted to make a point to bridge the gap between all Christian believers.

They all knew her from the community and they loved her dearly. It was always so spiritually gratifying when she was invited to get up and speak. Her simple language, her simple message of truth, her beautiful being, radiating God's truth from the inside. She had found her spiritual home at last.

Eighteen - Atlanta

Fear dominated the minds of the people as word spread that the Yankees were heading toward their city from the west. Atlanta was right in the path of General Sherman's march across Georgia. It was late in 1864 and the Civil War had entered its final chapter.

As a hub for southern railroads and as a manufacturing center, the city was an important strategic target for the Union. When Sherman captured it in September, he ordered its military resources, including munition factories, clothing mills and railway yards, burned to the ground. The fires got out of control and left Atlanta in ruins. Her people harbored a special intense hatred for the North for the century that followed.

After the war, Atlanta eventually rebuilt herself and became the flagship for the New South. She displaced the older cities like Savannah and Charleston and surpassed their prominence. But with failed Reconstruction and the rise of Jim Crow laws, she became a hotbed of racial discontent and civil strife.

Out of those turbulent decades, the modern era of the civil rights movement would be born. Its leaders would often be educated in theology and use the pulpit to preach the message of racial equality. Their hope would be that Christianity would solve the issue of racial prejudice as others in the past had hoped it would end slavery.

In 1948, a young man born in rural Georgia in 1929 earned his degree in sociology from the prestigious Morehouse College. He attended a prominent school of theology in Pennsylvania and graduated as the valedictorian in 1951. His doctorate came from Boston University in 1955 after completing his dissertation in 1954. He became impassioned with the civil rights cause and he too believed Christianity and peaceful protest would overcome the practice of segregation most prevalent in the South. His participation in the Southern Christian Leadership Conference with Ralph Abernathy would be a testament to his intended peaceful approach.

As a second generation freeborn man of mixed race raised in the North and in the Christian faith by his parents and his Aunt Hanna, Josiah Ashford II grew up with a special sense of self-awareness. His grandfather Josiah had been a slave and his mother was white.

He earned a dual degree in sociology and history from Miami of Ohio University and came to Atlanta in 1955 as a 38 year old man still in search of answers.

He met the young 26 year old newly ordained minister on the sidewalk outside a Baptist church. They spoke to each other as strangers who immediately felt like kindred spirits.

"Hello, my name is Josiah Ashford. My friends call me Joe", he said.

"It's a pleasure meeting you Joe. I'm Martin", the man replied.

They met often at a small restaurant down Jackson Street from Ebenezer Baptist Church. It was a run-down old place frequented by blacks in the segregated city. Martin loved the soul food – southern fried chicken and catfish, barbequed ribs, hocks, black eyed peas, buttered hominy grits and collard greens - the best of the south, especially the South Carolina low country food.

They talked about the problems of segregation and racial equality facing African Americans now, almost a hundred years after emancipation.

Joe told Martin he was mixed race. His mother was white.

Martin smiled to himself and told him, "Truth be told, most of us African Americans are mixed race. We just don't often know the whens and the whos and the whys so much."

Joe nodded his head.

"Seriously though Joe", he continued, "I pray every day. Some days more than once. Still I can't claim to know God's plan. Maybe he intends for the races to mix until we are all brown. Don't know."

"Don't know either", was all Joe could say.

"What I do know though, and I'm certain God would be right with it, is it's past the time when we should be kept separate and treated inferior by our white brothers", Martin offered.

"You should have known my grandfather Josiah and my aunt Hanna", Joe told him.

"Grampa was a slave and a freedman who built a furniture dynasty for our family up in southwest Ohio where I am from. I never knew him but heard he was a fierce man of God. He fought for our people but believed in friendship as the solution for the inhumanity of man."

Martin was pleased to hear stories like that. It fit with his passionate approach to life.

"Maybe the most important thing about his life Martin was his friend David, a white Civil War veteran. They supported each other every step of the way. David was troubled and Grampa tried to help him, tried to get him to know God. They were different in that way too. But they loved each other. David is buried right next to him."

Martin nodded his head with pleasure.

Finally Joe told him about Hanna. "You should have known my aunt Hanna. She was one of the last freed slaves when she passed a few years ago. Like you, she made her life a mission to serve God – maybe a mission to improve harmony between the races, more than equality. She did it well, peaceably and with love – down in Mississippi and up in Ohio. She helped raise me as a little boy and taught me all the bible stories."

"What about you?" Martin asked him.

"I am at a point in my life where I see the strife and cruelty in the country once again and I want to do something about it."

After they shared each other's life stories and got to know each other well, Joe came to a decision. He would follow the young Martin Luther King, Jr. to Montgomery, Alabama where King would become the pastor at the Dexter Avenue Baptist Church.

When Joe caught Martin's impassioned fire, he became enthusiastic and so excited he wrote his mother, Elizabeth Jefferson Ashford:

Dearest Mother,

I met the most magnificent man in Atlanta. His name is Martin Luther King, Jr. He is inspirational, and charismatic, almost messianic. You would love his mind and his spirit. He is of the purest heart and so smart.

He has a vision. He told me he has seen the mountain top. It is very steep and high though, Mother. Our people have so far to climb.

But Martin and I have so much in common, we are sympathetic souls. I plan to follow him on his mission and see where God's amazing grace will lead us.

Please take care to share this letter with father.

Warmest Love and Best Wishes,
Joe

Together they would spearhead the effort to de-segregate Montgomery's city bus system. They would be there to support the arrested protestor Claudette Colvin in March and later Rosa Parks in December in the citywide bus boycott.

Martin was, among many extraordinary things, a leader of men. He saw in Joe a valuable asset to his organization and movement. Joe had the right background and with his racial makeup, could help him bridge the racial gap.

While his old father continued to run the factory, Joe and his family's economic security had always been assured. Young Joe had joined with his mother Peggy and aunt Josena to further the cause. They continued the work begun by his grandfather before the turn of the century. Together they organized peaceful protests and petitioned the Ohio government to advance participation in suffrage, educational and job opportunity for people of color.

With renewed inspiration from Martin, Joe continued his work now on the national scene. His life's path was determined and he would remain Martin's loyal friend and by his side in Washington, DC for his historic speech and again on that tragic day in Memphis when Martin would be struck down by an assassin's bullet.

After Martin's passing, Joe remained active with the National Association for the Advancement of Colored People the rest of his life. He would return often to Ohio – to his home in Ashford and his campus in Oxford.

Joe carried on the work as his vocation – long into his mature years and made his mark as his grandfather had before him.

Years later, as an old man, he would become a frequent guest lecturer who would tell the young students there on the Miami of Ohio University campus about his grandfather Josiah and his aunt Hanna – about how they lived their lives and how they persevered and prevailed with grace over adversity.

Nineteen – Promise of the Future

When Josena Ashford went back to university in 1907 to get her Master's Degree in African studies – that is the study of the continent of Africa, its anthropology, its peoples and its sociology – she was confronted with a conflict between her faith and the new science of evolution. She resolved it easily and wrote about it in her book, *The Soul of Africa,* and taught it to her students at Miami of Ohio University, this way:

In the beginning, the Creator created the whole of the universe out of nothingness in an instant with a bang. As it is written, he created all of it in six days and then rested the seventh.

By the end of the fifth day, He had created the firmaments and the heavens, the stars and the planets and the Earth. Upon the Earth, the oceans and the land were in place. The seeds of the land had produced the lush green fields and the forests and the mountains. The beasts were bountiful in all of the Earth's places.

We think of those days as we are accustomed to thinking about time. We speak of them as the Creator's days. But the Creator's clock and time is not the same as ours. What for Him was one day, would have been hundreds of thousands of years to us had we been there as an observer.

He then turned His attention on the sixth day to the creation of man. In Africa, He created man in His image. Throughout the long day He made many adjustments.

The tall grass of the savannah required that man stand upright to see above it. His body shape and skeleton were adjusted so that he could rotate his shoulders, grasp with his opposable thumbs to hold tools that he fashioned, and throw a spear at his prey.

His skin was as dark as possible to block the strong sun but still allow its vitamin D to nourish him. After a while, some men courageously crossed the Red Sea and left Africa to explore the rest of the Earth. They spread throughout the Middle East, Europe and Asia and crossed the ice bridge over the Bering Strait from Siberia to North and South America.

They had learned to sew and fashion warm clothing from the furs of animals they had killed to keep them warm and insure their survival in the colder climate of the age. Later, after the ice age was over, the ice bridge went away and the native peoples of the Americas were isolated by the vast oceans until the future time when others would be able to cross them.

To survive in the ice age, the pigment of those that left had to be adjusted for their survival. They became lighter and paler to still get vitamin D from the weaker sun, but without as much need for protection from its rays. Other than that adjustment, and a couple other minor adjustments like that, man was exactly the same. There was no need for further adjustments.

The Creator continued His work until the whole of the Earth was populated with man by the end of that long day. And then, tired, He rested.

After His work was done, He gave man free will and autonomy on the Earth. Much remained the same in Africa. Life was simple and basic. Eventually man formed family units and then communities and then villages and then tribes. The trouble began.

Some of her students took the meaning of this, but some did not. There was an inexplicable recalcitrance, even an irony, in some minds. There were some ignorant poor whites who viewed educated successful blacks as inferior. It was almost like a jealously as well as a bigotry.

Josie had always felt that intellectually, beyond emotionality, there was a stupidity in their non-thinking way that went beyond reason; yet the stupidity was there all the same. She wondered and considered, 'God knows how Hanna could so gracefully work around it, push through it, and most often change peoples' hearts.'

He does. He knew that the meek like Hanna could melt their hardened heats and turn their hatred to love.

Yahweh, the Creator of the Universe, had used His mighty power in past millennia to punish the wicked. The people held Him in such awe, they dared not speak His name.

Jehovah, the keeper of the Heavens, had spoken directly to the Prophets to compel them to warn the people. God had sent His angels as messengers to inspire hope and provide reassurance. God, the Eternal Spirit of Love, had even sent a Son to teach by example and sacrifice.

Giving His creations free will had limited His power. He had seen what worked and what didn't. He was still adjusting. He developed better plans as He lived through His eighth day and began His second week.

Josena reconciled the apparent conflict between creationism and evolution in that way. It would be a few more years before the controversy on this subject would explode across American education. It was a contest between theology and modern science.

In 1925, a high school teacher named John Thomas Scopes would be brought to trial for teaching Darwin's theory of evolution in the classroom. He was in violation of Tennessee's Butler Act which made it illegal to teach that subject in state funded schools. William Jennings Bryan argued for the prosecution and Clarence Darrow for the defense. In the end, Scopes was found guilty and fined $100, but the verdict was overturned on a technicality.

But Josena was teaching about more than that in her classes at University of Miami. She was arguing, as she always would, against Social Darwinism as well. She rejected, and made it clear, that the notion of the inherent inferiority of people of color was nonsense. She based her assertions on the anthropological evidence of the origin of man – in Africa. The white man was a derivative of the black man and therefore could not be superior. She knew this even if others did not.

One day when Josena was off her duties at Miami of Ohio University, she and Hanna went over to Ashford Furniture to visit David in his office. Somehow the conversation with his sisters turned to Abraham Lincoln and his presidency.

Hanna offered, "Ya know Abe Lincoln, he free our people. God blessed us with his life."

"That is true Hanna, but the way it came about was not that simple. He was just a man after all.", Josena replied.

David thought about the conversation, sensed Josena's meaning and launched into one of his lectures. It was a long one but informative and insightful.

"When I was a young boy David Wexley told me after the war he had thought about it. Here in Ohio, he had many years to reflect on his experiences and their meanings for him. His father had discussed many things about slavery and our politics with him before the war, but this was after it and his own reflections. He studied it as a man who was there and needed to know more about the men he had never known like Lincoln and Grant and Lee.

He told me that in the middle of the war, some twenty months since it began at Fort Sumter, President Lincoln was in trouble. He was struggling to preserve the Union up to that point. Emancipation of the slaves would come later. The war had come to a halt and a stalemate. Both sides were entrenched holding their gains and not moving forward.

Lincoln was beset with so many problems just then; he was alternately standing still, moving forward and making mistakes, and constantly changing strategy trying to end it. His generals were pulling him in all directions. The American people of the Union were out of patience and despondent from the loss of blood and treasure and time. They blamed it all on him.

His own Republicans in Congress, the Radical ones, and the newspapers were constantly harassing him, calling him an ignorant and incompetent fool. Even some members of his own cabinet were against him. But he persevered and spent his time thinking and writing. He believed he could convince them if he could just craft the most compelling words.

He had written a preliminary Emancipation Proclamation but his Secretary of State, William Seward advised him to put it in a drawer until the time was right. He taught Lincoln that timing was everything.

When he released it, the time was right. You might not believe this, but freeing the slaves was not its purpose. He had learned the skill of politics and the Proclamation would benefit him and the federal government fourfold.

First, it would not offend the tenuous relationship he held with the Union border-states – Delaware, Kentucky, Maryland and Missouri - who held slaves. They would be allowed to keep their slaves.

Second, it would not free slaves in the north – in the Union. He wanted to appease certain members of Congress. It only freed slaves in Union controlled Confederate states.

Third, he needed replenishment of troops by then and black freedmen could serve in the Union army.

Fourth, and not much known, he was constantly competing with Jefferson Davis for foreign sympathy and support in England and France. They needed the South's cotton but hated its slavery. Lincoln hoped this would fool them and sway them to the Union side. It might not have been convincing to some overseas who saw through to its veiled purposes, but at least it kept them from swinging to Jefferson Davis's side. Lincoln was walking a tightrope.

About that time, Lincoln came into his own. He had begun master-crafting those compelling words he needed. In his December message to Congress, a long fifty thousand words delivered by a moderator in his absence, it began with a blessing followed by well- wishing, a grieving about the war, and launched into a long host of boring humdrum matters. It was a dry beginning.

After nearly losing them, it began to hit its stride at mid-point when the tone changed.

He wrote, "A nation may be said to consist of its territory, its people, and its laws. The territory is the only part which is of certain durability. 'One generation passeth away, and another generation cometh: but the earth abideth forever.' It is of the first importance to duly consider and estimate this ever-enduring part. That portion of the earth's surface which is owned and inhabited by the people of the United States is well adapted to be the home of one national family, and it is not well adapted for two or more.... There is no line, straight or crooked, suitable for a national boundary upon which to divide. Trace through, from east to west, upon the line between the free and slave country, and we shall find a little more than one-third of its length are rivers, easy to be crossed and populated, or soon to be populated, thickly upon both sides; while nearly all its remaining lengths are merely surveyors' lines, over which people may walk back and forth without any consciousness of their presence."

What he was getting at and talking about here was his own native, interior, land-locked, region needing access to seacoasts and ports for the good of the nation.

He added further that, "Our national strife springs not from our permanent part, not from the land we inhabit, not from our national homestead.... Our strife pertains to ourselves – to the passing generations of men; and it can without convulsion be hushed forever with the passing of one generation."

This brought him at last to the heart of the matter in his mind when he wrote, "Without slavery the rebellion could never have existed; without slavery it could not continue."

His last words to the Congressmen on this occasion were, "..... The fiery trial through which we pass will light us down, in honor or dishonor, to the latest generation. We say we are for the Union. The world will not forget that we say this. We know how to save the Union. The world knows we do know how to save it. We – even we here – hold the power and bear the responsibility. In giving freedom to the slave, we assure freedom to the free – honorable alike in what we give and what we preserve. We shall nobly save or meanly lose the last, best hope of earth. Other means may succeed; this could not fail. The way is plain, peaceful, generous, just – a way which, if followed, the world will forever applaud, and God must forever bless."

David told me that the cost for what Mr. Lincoln was requesting was immeasurably great. Of course "we here" would not be able to do anything to assure anything he said. It would have to be done by young men who are farmers or teachers or merchants and follow old generals into battle.

He questioned whether the incalculable price was worth it. After all he have seen on the ground, it pained him to consider it glory. He still believed it was right, but said there is no glory. No glory whatsoever.

He recalled that the commanding officers talked about glory. They were doing their job – what they were trained to do – getting us to march, to entrench, to stand up to withering fire from artillery and muskets, to charge with clashing bayonets, to staunch the bleeding, to bury the dead. There is no glory, just aggression meeting aggression.

Some called them killer angels. He never saw it that way. It may have been about honor. He did not know. It was not noble. Our father tried to help him understand it and bring him peace through his God. David was not a Godly man. From my experiences in World War I, I understand David Wexley better than either of you ever can."

David Ashford looked back at the war before he was born as an historian would. He learned and understood the politics of how Lincoln's and David Wexley's Civil War was going. The months following the Emancipation Proclamation, the number of visitors to the people's house increased. In those days, visitors had generally free access to an audience with the President and the Secret Service was not highly focused on security.

Abolitionists were generally pleased with Lincoln's performance and his popularity began to turn for the better. His political strategies for public support were working. The progress with the war however, had much to be improved.

Lincoln was pained to break the law – the Constitution – as he saw it while he suspended Writs of Habeas Corpus and invoked conscription. The poor Irish in the North were embittered about the new draft laws of military service and embittered further with being forced to fight for the Negro cause – not to mention the threat of free Negroes taking away their employment.

David Ashford, as well as David Wexley before then, understood that Lincoln had continued to be beleaguered. Josena Ashford had continued to follow it the years later when her brother had studied it, but Hanna had no idea. That was probably for the best because it wouldn't have helped her. It would have confused her and stood in the way of her divine mission.

Josena and Peggy were away at the university most days; so Hanna took care of baby Joe. Before she passed away, while David was overseas, Mary spent her last days with pleasure and satisfaction watching them from her rocking chair.

Over the years Hanna became the boy's companion and as he grew older, she read him the exciting stories in the bible. He loved the stories of Samson and Delilah, Daniel in the lion's den, Jonah in the belly of the whale, and old Noah saving the animals from the flood.

Hanna loved telling him, "Now Josiah, when Joshua fit the battle of Jericho, he free his people. 'N' old Moses led his people out of Egypt to be free in the Promised Land. Abraham Lincoln, he free our people."

He smiled at Aunt Hanna's face and remembered every word.

Some days, with little to do, Hanna accompanied Josena to Oxford in Josena's Ford motor car. While Josena taught her classes there at Miami of Ohio University, Hanna spent her day on campus watching and listening to the young students. She heard some strong emotional diatribes of racial injustice and some vitriolic language of racial prejudice. The arguments fell just short of physical violence.

When she could she engaged the students. "I'm an old wuman that has seen a lotta cruelty in my life in the South. I've seen kindness too from people you wouldn't expect. The best I can tells y'all is right in the good book. Love is patient, love is kind. It does not envy, it does not boast, it is not proud. It is not rude, it is not self-seeking, it is not easily angered, it keeps no record of wrongs. Love does not delight in evil, but rejoices with the truth. It always protects, always trusts, always hopes, always perseveres."

Eyes shining with passionate faith and glistening aglow with abiding love, arms raised outstretched with upturned palms, body bent beckoning toward them, she smiled at them and said, "Love is not just a feelin', it's a choice and an action and a blessing."

Most listened to her, many smiled, some wanted to believe, some decided and were profoundly affected and came to her and took her hands and knew love.

David too was trying to resolve issues in his mind from his life's experience and it was time for another brainstorming session with his sister, Josena. It began, as it often did, with him delivering her a lecture.

He told her, "History is transitory. And it is generally cyclical, but manifesting itself differently with each cycle. It is like a mutating organism."

Darwinism dominated the intellectual thinking at the time.

"Its truth", he continued, "is there but illusive and temporary. You can never wrap your arms around it and hold it still long enough to draw ultimate conclusions.

From its multitude of little ideas, you can draw only a misty vision of the biggest ideas. But it is the only teacher that we have."

Josena responded, "Hanna would tell you that there is a better teacher, one we can learn from with certainty after all our intellect is exhausted."

He knew what she meant by that; the conversation became silent while he pondered what she had said.

At this point in his mature life, David had grown to have doubt in his faith. As he most often did, he turned to his twin sister again.

"I don't believe I am a Christian in every sense. I mean I believe in God, His creation and Providence, but I'm not convinced of all the tenants of Jesus Christ. I haven't made the leap of faith or the final commitment.

Maybe it is because of what I have lived, learned and seen – all of man's inhumanity, father's early life and those before him. I can't believe in altruism for its own sake. Charity is goodness, but it must be voluntary not demanded. I will help people because I believe it is right, but never if it is somehow expected of me.

Hanna is surely different. She has the faith. She follows the command to love as her purpose in life. God bless her for that."

Josena tried to grasp her brother's belief and said, "But David that is not what we were raised to believe. I am surprised. I don't believe you have changed like that."

"I believe in the individual, in the pursuit of one's happiness, as the founders of our country believed", he said. "It looks as if their ideals are beginning to be realized for the rest of us at long last. Now we must look out for our own, our people, our family."

She reflected on that and replied, "And our country David. For the good of us all."

"I'm not so sure about that", he responded.

"War changes a man. Look at David Wexley."

"What do you mean by that?", she asked him.

"Before we went to war, we had such moral certainty. We were idealistic, everything was clear – simple. War changes all that. We hope to return not just to our families, but to the man we once were. I'm not certain how to answer you any better than that.

David Wexley tried to pursue his happiness, but somehow he failed to realize it. It is very complicated and confusing."

She offered, "Well a man's life is the best he can make it. David Wexley made a difference in the world. Hanna has too. I think you should talk to Hanna."

"Thanks Josie. I'm sure you are right", he answered.

One summer evening, he stood on the porch looking across the yard at Hanna. She was sitting on the old family bench under the oak tree. In the netherworld between day and night, Hanna was looking at the sky – dark blue with a pale moon and the North star visible at the same time as the daylight.

He walked over and stood next to her beside the bench, staring out at the broad sky with her.

"What is it David?", she asked him.

"I have been trying to think about God and the meaning of all this", he gestured to the panorama.

"Sit down brother."

Without conversation, or need for it, he sat down next to her and took her right hand in his left. They sat there together for a while, looking ahead, tears flowing down David's cheeks.

She turned toward him and smiling at him, placed her left hand on top of his.

They looked at each other lovingly and with a poignancy of understanding. He felt a gentle tingle – a pulsation – flowing up his arm and throughout his body, and he knew.

He knew for the first time what she knew. He had not learned of it in college, in the factory, from his father, overseas, on the road across America, or in Ohio - had only a glimpse of it when his son had been born. It was the ultimate and real truth.

It was how she had survived, endured, surmounted, prevailed, didn't need to be endlessly searching, found happiness. The face of God was inside him, before his mind, a part of him, for the first time a certainty, a permanent unshakable truth never to be taken away.

One Sunday David attended the AME Church. As a prominent member of the community and its chief employer, he was welcomed – welcomed out of respect and yes curiosity too.

There was an interesting dynamic in the churches in the town of Hamilton and the little village of Ashford. From all the years that Hanna had been there, with her influence on all the people of the community and the Ashford family as the primary employer for the area – essentially the founders of Ashford, Ohio - the churches were attended mostly evenly by both races. It was odd that so many whites attended the African Methodist Episcopal Church and so many blacks the Presbyterian Church, but that was how it was. The division was more along the lines of class. The poorer people who earned the lower wages tended toward the AME congregation, whereas the more affluent tended toward the Presbyterian one.

So is was a bit unusual for David to show up at the AME Church with his wife Peggy and son Joe; more so than Hanna. They sat all together as a family.

David asked the pastor if he would be allowed to speak a few words to the congregation. The pastor nodded to him with a smile in the affirmative. This once David's words were short and, on this occasion, a heartfelt prayer.

"Pray with me", he said. "Dear Lord, I want to give my thanks for all You have given me in my blessed life, my wife Peggy who with her love and devotion, has been my partner in breaking down the barriers of color here in our beloved community of Ashford and Hamilton, our son Joe who we know will be the hope for our future and last and most of all our dear sister Hanna – sister to our family, our community and yes even many parts of our country.

Her life and love and inspiration has been the greatest blessing I have seen God bring into our lives. And for me, she has shown me the right way to live and to be and made me free at last. For all these things and people, I thank you Lord."

"Once a great King David pleased the Lord. Here is David's confidence in God's grace. A Psalm of David. Pray with me the words of his 23rd Psalm in the good book where we are taught to give praise to His name –

The Lord is my shepherd, I shall not want.

He maketh me to lie down in green pastures: he leadeth me beside the still waters.

He restoreth my soul: he leadeth me in the path of righteousness for his name's sake.

Yea, though I walk through the valley of the shadow of death, I will fear no evil: for thou art with me; thy rod and thy staff they comfort me.

Thou preparest a table before me in the presence of mine enemies; thou annoitest my head with oil; my cup runneth over.

Surely goodness and mercy shall follow me all the days of my life: and I will dwell in the house of the Lord for ever."

The pastor embraced him before he returned to his place with his family.

After all the years living with her father and the Ashfords, Hanna Drish never changed her last name. It was given to her by her adoptive white parents, John and Sarah and she would forever honor their love for her.

When she passed away during the throes of World War II, the town commissioned a bronze statue of her and placed it in the center of the square there in Ashford, Ohio.

The plaque at the base of the statue was inscribed:

Hanna Drish (1856-1942) – slave, freedwoman, healer of hearts, beloved sister to our community.

David and Josena were there for the commemoration, along with David's wife Peggy and their son. The community remembered her as their historical heroine for generations and to this day. She was known as the woman credited for the extraordinary racial harmony enjoyed in that region. Miami of Ohio history school included her life story in their classes. She had kept her promise.

Epilogue

By November of 1942, America had been at war again for almost a year. The Japanese had attacked in the Pacific and captured the Philippines by then. While fighting them there, America was preparing to fight the Germans on a second front in Europe. Once again the world was coming apart. God was saddened and grew more tired still, now that he was older.

On the 25th of that month and year, Hanna Drish left this mortal coil. Josena sat next to her on her bed and held her in her arms. David was in her room watching from the rocking chair. They waited quietly. No one spoke.

Hanna's face was serene. The lines of care were gone and her skin seemed to glow with a lambency, inexplicably brighter than the ambient light that filled the room from the late afternoon sun coming through the lace curtains of the window.

Josena watched as soundless tears ran down her cheeks. She was remembering how Hanna had sung the words to her that Hanna's mother Josena had sung to her as a child – those sweet words from *God Bless the Child* and *Swing Low Sweet Chariot.* As she remembered, she hummed them softly and gently rocked Hanna.

Hanna's eyes opened and she looked at her sister one last time before they flickered and closed. Josena smiled as she watched Hanna's chest heave and exhale her last breath. David heard the last rush of air as his sister became motionless – more still than a living person could possibly be.

She was gone. Only her motionless body lie silently in the bed. Her work was done. She went home. For that moment, God was happy. He was pleased and He was smiling. His Hanna would be with Him very soon.

David looked out the window at the golden sun sparkling on the fresh snow just fallen on the ground in the fields of Hamilton. The air was crisp. It smelled new and seemed to offer promise and hope.

At that same moment, white billowy clouds, with golden fringes from the glorious late afternoon sun, were moving rapidly across the sky in Alabama over the patch of Earth where she was born. One of the smallest of them had a golden brilliance more than the others.

Michael's wings were spread wide and his arms were folded tightly around the embodiment of Hanna's immortal soul as he climbed higher and higher until he was just a pinpoint barely visible or discernible or comprehendible to any person on the ground.

And Grace had led her home.

end

Characters

Yahweh, Jehovah, God, the Creator of the Universe

Michael – Archangel from the South of Fire

Hanna Drish – freedwoman from Drish plantation, daughter of Josiah and Josena Ashford

Josiah Ashford - slave and freedman, Savannah Oaks plantation

Josena Taylor Ashford - Josiah's wife and a slave, Savannah Oaks and Drish plantations

Mary Custis Ashford - Josiah's 2nd wife

David Custis Ashford, Josena Custis Ashford - Josiah's children, Hanna Drish's half siblings

David Wexley – friend of the Ashfords

Dr. John and Sarah Drish – Owners of Drish plantation near Tuscaloosa, Alabama

Kenneth and Abigail Blanchard – Wealthy merchants in Mobile, Alabama

Nora Travers, Hanna's friend

Elizabeth Jefferson – David Ashford's wife

Sam Jefferson – Elizabeth's father

Crista and Hans Hannon – migrants to Ashford, Ohio

Locations

Hamilton, Ohio – Ashford family farm and estate

Tuscaloosa, Alabama - John Drish Plantation

Mobile, Alabama – Hanna Drish's adopted home

Montgomery, Alabama – First capital of the Confederacy

Atlanta, Georgia – Industrial center of the South

McComb, Mississippi - town where Hanna settled

Buffalo, New York – City where the Hannons were from

Character and Historical Timeline

1795 - John Drish is born in Virginia

1807- Marcus Taylor is born in Savannah

1809 - Rebecca Stanley is born in Charleston

1820 - Missouri Compromise

1822 - John Drish came to Tuscaloosa and bought 450 acre property

1829 - Josiah Ashford is born on a Missouri plantation

1832 - David Wexley is born in Baltimore

1837- Josena is born on Savannah Oaks plantation

1837 - Drish House completed

1852 - Marcus bought Josiah for his Savannah Oaks plantation

1853 - Josiah and Josena marry on Savannah Oaks

1854 - The Kansas-Nebraska Act

1856 - Josena is sold from Savannah Oaks to Drish plantation

1856 - Hanna, Josena's daughter, is born on Drish plantation

1860 - Lincoln elected President, South Carolina secedes

1861 - The Civil War breaks out

1864 - Josena is killed on Drish plantation

1864 - Hanna, age 8 is sent to the Blanchard family in Mobile,

Alabama to raise her and care for her

1865 - Lee surrenders to Grant at Appomattox, April 9th

1865 - Lincoln assassinated in Ford's theater, April 14th

1865- Joe Johnston surrenders to Sherman at Durham Station NC, April 26th

1865 - 13th Amendment passed abolishing slavery

1865 - Josiah is freed and meets David Wexley in Natchez, Mississippi

1866 - KKK supported by Confederate General Nathan Bedford Forrest to terrorize the South

1867 - John Drish died in an accidental fall

1868 - Josiah meets Mary Custis in Hamilton, Ohio

1869 - Josiah and Mary give birth to twins – David Custis Ashford and Josena Custis Ashford

1869 - Hanna, age 13 meets the Archangel, Michael in her Mobile, Alabama home

1877- Post-war reconstruction abandoned

1881 - Marcus dies in McComb, Mississippi

1882 - Hanna, age 26 comes to McComb and cares for old crazy Rebecca

1884 - Sarah Drish died

1887 – Public schools in Ohio are integrated

1888 - Rebecca dies, Hanna buries her

1892 - The twins, David and Josena graduate from Oberlin College

1898 - Spanish American war (David is 29)

1900 - The twins, age 31 travel south, retrace some of Josiah and David's old route

1900 - The twins unite with Hanna, age 44 in McComb

1900 - Telephone transmission extends across and between major cities

1900 - David Wexley dies in Aspen, Colorado

1900 - The twins return to Hamilton with Hanna and for David Wexley's burial

1903-1909 - Wright brothers in Dayton, Ohio develop flying machine

1906 - Drish House converted to a school, Drish property sub-divided

1906 - Josiah dies in Hamilton, Ohio

1906 - Hanna gets close to Mary and cares for her

1907 – David runs Ashford Furniture, Josena (38) attends Miami of Ohio for her master's degree

1908 - Henry Ford introduces first viable gasoline powered automobile

1909 – NAACP founded by W.E.B. DuBois

1910 – Josena introduces Peggy Jefferson to David

1912 - Woodrow Wilson elected President, social Darwinist racist who liked Birth of a Nation

1912 – David (43) marries Peggy Jefferson (34)

1915 – David and Peggy have a son

1915 - The Birth of a Nation movie debuts

1917 - The United States enters World War I

1917 - David enlists in U.S. Army as a correspondent with 93nd division under BG Roy Hoffman

1917 - Mary dies while David is overseas, Josena, Peggy and Hanna bury Mary

1918 - David returns from the war and reunites with Peggy, his son (3) and sisters

1918 - David and Josena again revitalize and run Ashford Furniture Company

1918-1942 – Hanna (62-86) serves the community and becomes a legendary figure for unification and harmony

1920 - 19th Amendment ratified for woman's suffrage

1925 – The Scopes Monkey Trial in Dayton, Tennessee

1929 – Martin Luther King, Jr. born in Atlanta, Georgia

1942 - Hanna dies at 86, David and Josena are 73 with her in Hamilton, Ohio

1968 – Martin Luther King, Jr. assassinated in Memphis, Tennessee

1968 – Josiah Ashford II, David's son, frequents Miami of Ohio Campus

Ashford Family Tree

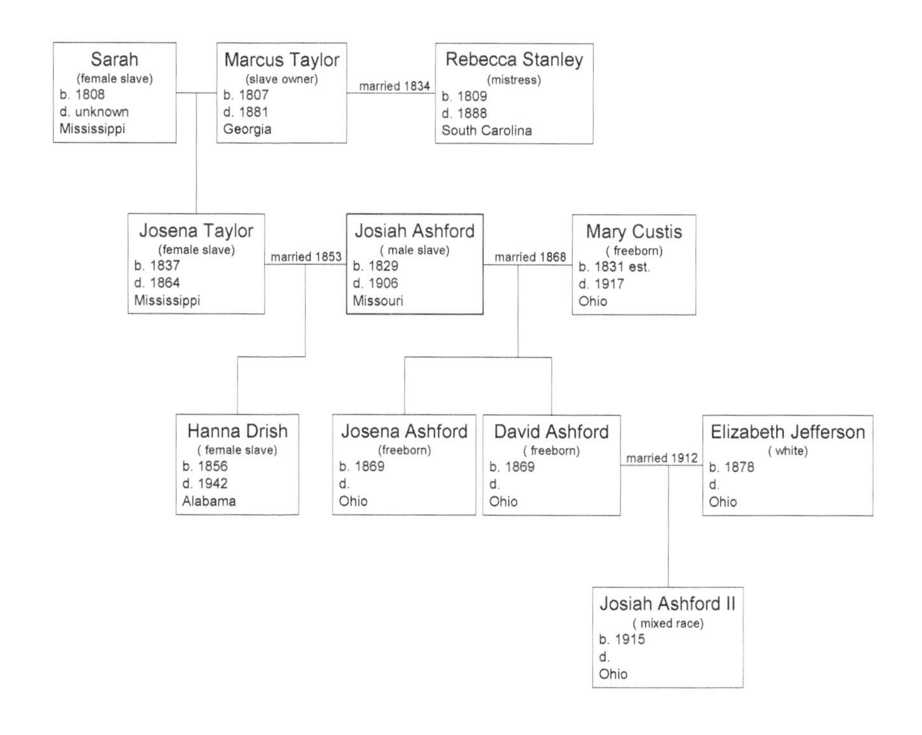